IT BEGAN WITH A PATTERN
OF INCONSISTENCIES . . .

Item: That kitten's tail had been prehensile—the way a monkey's tail was supposed to be, not a cat's.

Item: Canute could climb a tree—catlike.

Item: John had never been out of the township.

Item: Some of his schoolmates had skin that could peel off, like furniture varnish. Underneath it was tan. John's skin would not peel; it became tan in summer but faded to a pale color in winter.

Item: His parents didn't like him to remark on such things.

. . . AND LED TO A DEADLY

Look for this other TOR book by Piers Anthony

PRETENDER (written by Piers Anthony and Frances Hall)

PIERS ANTHONY
RACE AGAINST TIME

A TOM DOHERTY ASSOCIATES BOOK

RACE AGAINST TIME

Copyright © 1973 by Piers Anthony

A TOR Book

Published by Tom Doherty Associates
8-10 West 36 Street
New York, N.Y. 10018

First TOR printing: September 1985

ISBN: 0-812-53110-8
CAN. ED.: 0-812-53111-6

Printed in the United States of America

Contents

1

Three
Wishes

Canute raced ahead as John skirted the overgrown pasture. The grass was waist high and ready for cutting. There were perpetual rustles within it, leading the dog a happy chase.

"One man went to mow," John sang, slightly off-key, "went to mow the meadow. One man and his dog went to mow the meadow."

Canute, thinking he was being called, returned to peer at his master inquiringly. His brow was wrinkled vertically, one ear was inside out, and there was a bit of dirt on his nose.

"Two men went to mow, went to mow the meadow," John continued, patting the dog affectionately. "Two men, one man, and his dog went to mow the meadow."

Canute heard something and shot away into the grass again, tail wagging.

"Three men went to mow. . . ."

John was up to twelve men—and a dog—by the time he reached the spruce grove. Canute rejoined him, sniffing this new ground as avidly as ever. The layered needles were spongy, the air abruptly still. John reflected that he must have been here a thousand times, and the dog a hundred, yet there was always something to intrigue the human mind and the canine nose.

Had been something. John realized that today he was bored with it and had in fact been bored for some time without being aware of it. Everything in the township was overfamiliar. He knew every house, every yard, every tree of the surrounding countryside. He stopped beside the largest tree. Most of its lower branches had been broken off, leaving dead spokes or sappy wounds in the trunk. He would get filthy if he climbed it.

So he climbed it, hoisting himself by hand and foot. Canute paced worriedly beneath, his spotty forehead wrinkling again. The dog did not like to be left alone, even for a few seconds. Though sleek and hefty, he was at six months still a puppy. He demanded a lot of attention and usually got it. He could howl soulfully and with considerable volume when neglected.

John paused to peer down. Canute was standing against the trunk, his paws against the lowest spoke, head tilted back appealingly. One black spot impinged on an eye, making him seem lopsided, and his open mouth showed pink and black. He began to whine.

"Well, come on up!" John called.

Canute watched him, tail wagging hopefully.

"Up! Up the tree, mutt," John said, smiling.

The dog fidgeted, making his spots ripple. He whined louder and added a yip. Then suddenly he curved his front paws around the spoke, scrambled with his hind legs, and pulled himself up.

"You can do it!" John cried. "Keep climbing, boy!"

Canute struggled upward. As he ascended, he gained proficiency, until he was making fair progress.

John resumed his own journey. "I'll race you, pooch!" he called.

At first he outdistanced the dog. Then, as the narrowing trunk and thicker foliage inhibited him, the gap between them shortened. By the time there was visibility above the small forest they were almost together. John noted with interest that Canute's paws no longer wrapped around the branches. Instead, his claws dug into the main trunk, retracting when he let go to find higher purchase. No wonder he could climb faster!

The tree swayed. "We'd better stop," John gasped. "Top might snap off." He didn't really believe that, of course . . . then another gust of wind touched them, and he *did* believe.

They stopped, clinging to opposite sides of the

slender trunk. From this vantage, with head and tail out of sight, Canute looked very much like a leopard. John wondered fleetingly whether Dalmatians had any leopard blood. No—leopards were basically cats, he was sure; they couldn't interbreed with dogs.

"I didn't know dogs could climb," he said as an afterthought. "Well, let's go down before we're late for supper."

Canute, always ready for food, needed no coaxing. He backed down, those marvelous claws operating smoothly. John had to hurry to keep the pace. It bothered him, though. He *hadn't* known that dogs could climb trees.

They dusted themselves off at the bottom and trotted on toward home. Mom was cooking supper. Green beans and chicken, the smell announced before they entered. Every second Tuesday, the same. He had memorized the schedule long ago.

It occurred to him to ask Mom about the tree-climbing ability of dogs, but he reconsidered immediately. Three years ago, when he was thirteen, he had had a kitten. The little cat had had a prehensile tail. John hadn't realized that this was remarkable until he researched cats in the encyclopedia and found no reference to this characteristic in felines. He had mentioned this to Mom, just as a matter of passing curiosity, but she had been quite upset. Next morning the cat was gone, never to return, and questions about its fate were turned aside. John had become more cautious about his remarks thereafter.

No—he would keep silent about Canute's talent. He liked the big dog too well to have him disappear abruptly.

He went up to his room and started to clean it while Canute chewed contentedly on an old shoe. John was not addicted to neatness, as the entrenched mess attested; he just needed time to think things over.

Canute's ability, John realized as he poked the broom under the bed and stirred up curly dust mice, followed a pattern of sorts—a pattern of little inconsistencies. The Smiths were an ordinary family, Newton was an ordinary town, and the United States was America. But:

Item: That kitten's tail had been prehensile—the way a monkey's tail was supposed to be, not a cat's.

Item: Canute could climb a tree—catlike.

Item: John had never been out of the township.

Item: Some of his schoolmates had skin that could peel off, like furniture varnish. Underneath it was tan. John's skin would not peel; it became tan in summer but faded to a pale color in winter.

Item: His parents didn't like him to remark on such things.

That was enough for a start. Five items—was there a consistent framework for these things? A common explanation? A ripple of goose pimples went up his arms and across his shoulders and on into the back of his head. He was not cold; that was the way he reacted to discovery. Five items—and suddenly he was certain they *were* linked! The connection was really fundamental, affecting his entire outlook, maybe his life.

Mom appeared. "Dear, have you written to Betsy yet?"

Someone always interrupted him when he started to *think*! It never failed.

"Not yet, Mom," he said, glancing at her with frustration. She was verging on fifty and getting stout; her hair was inclining toward gray. She had a round affectionate face, and her hands were wrinkled. Would they also peel if scratched?

"Maybe I'd better get started, though," he added quickly. "I was just thinking about her." That was a lie, but he didn't care to admit the true direction of his thoughts.

"That's good, John," she said. "Supper in fifteen minutes. Be sure to wash your hands." She left.

John looked at Betsy's picture, propped on his cluttered desk.

Item: He was going steady with a girl he had never met.

Well, now he was committed to that chore. He would have to write to Betsy Jones. Mom would fret if he didn't.

He brushed aside comics, magazines, and wood carvings to make a space for his typewriter. This was a battered portable with a broken bell and faded ribbon, but it worked well enough. He had taught himself to type by hunting and pecking with gradually increasing facility. He could now type slightly faster than he could write, and that was adequate. His composition was limited more by the speed of his thoughts than of his two fingers. He rolled through a sheet of paper and typed the date: August 12, 1960. Then, "Dear Betsy."

About then his mind went blank. What should a sixteen-year-old boy say to a sixteen-year-old girl he had never seen in his life? He had written to her every week for the past six months, but that didn't help. It meant only that he had exhausted the possibilities in routine description and query. In reply he had her weekly letters describing *her* house (pretty much like his), *her* town (ditto), *her* family, pet (a parakeet), school studies. She had to be as bored with it all as he. By mutual and unwritten consent they had never discussed romance. This contact had been arranged by their parents, and neither John nor Betsy could work up any enthusiasm for it. Probably the letters were snooped on, anyway.

John touched the keys without depressing them. How about: "Dear Betsy—how many inconsistent items can you count? Do your friends have the same fake white skin mine do?" Sure—if he really wanted to convince her he was crazy!

He picked up the picture, less for inspiration than to justify his failure to get on with the missive. She was a rather pretty girl, brown-haired, brown-eyed, cute curved nose, small mouth. In fact it would have been easy enough to like her had she been *here* instead of *there* and had she not been forced on him.

John liked to make his own decisions, such as they were. He had precious little opportunity. His school curriculum had been set by others, his homelife was ordered by his parents, and his summer wanderings were circumscribed by the township limits. About the only real freedoms he had were in his mind and heart. Unfortunately he did not have enough information to think really independently and had little interest in girls. That did not affect the principle. Certainly he was not about to get sloppy about Betsy Jones. Now or ever.

"Dear, are you feeling well?" Mom inquired.

He jumped. She was catlike on those stairs—no sound at all! "It's hard to say anything to a girl I've never met," he said lamely.

"You *will* meet her, John. When you graduate."

"But that's a year off!" He made it sound impatient. Actually he didn't care if it was a century.

"I know it's hard, dear. But it is for the best." She left again.

For the best? *Whose* best? Why did it have to be this way? Why these empty motions of remote-control courtship? He glanced at Canute, now snoozing on the rug. It was all part of the mystery— the girl, the dog, the cat, the fake skin, the subtle supervision. How could he unriddle it all, let alone overcome it?

He unfolded Betsy's last letter. She had waxed

philosophic, and he had only skimmed it disinterestedly upon receipt a couple of days ago. Did Betsy find this charade as frustrating as he did? Had she expressed her rebellion by writing high-sounding nonsense?

"Dear John," she had written. "Have you ever wondered what you would do if you had just three wishes? Three fairy-tale wishes, I mean, that you could make once and never again, and they could never be changed afterward. And whatever you phrased as a wish would be honored literally, even if it were only 'I wish I didn't have so much homework' or 'I wish you'd shut up.' And you couldn't cheat by wishing for a thousand more wishes or half a wish at one time."

Pointless speculation, but now that he considered her remarks at leisure, they did make some sense. He *had* dreamed about wishes, deciding what he might do with one wish or a hundred. He had decided that if one wish were used to ask for a thousand wishes, each of those would be only one-thousandth the strength of the first, so nothing could be gained. So he established a standard format of three medium-potent wishes; no more and no fewer could be used. When he was eight, he had settled on a toy store, a candy store, and a pet shop. At twelve it had been a spaceship (he had seen the design in a science-fiction magazine), a billion dollars in gold coin, and a purebred Dalmatian puppy.

Actually, it was high time he updated that list.

Like a last will and testament, the latest edition remained in force until superseded. He wasn't at all certain the wishes of a twelve-year-old boy should be binding on a young man. He no longer wanted the spaceship, since his interest in stellar navigation had waned. Gold coin was passé; an unlimited charge account would be better and far easier to carry around. And the Dalmatian he had now.

He returned to Betsy's letter: "At first I thought money or material possessions would make the ideal wish. But before long I realized that I have all of that sort of thing I need. My folks take care of me, clothe me, feed me; I have an allowance to cover other things. A million dollars would not make me happier, and it might make me sadder.

"Then I thought that all I had to wish for, really, was happiness itself. Nothing else means anything without that, and *with* it I would be independent of the other things. If wealth were a legitimate part of happiness, I would automatically have wealth; if residence in a palace were required, I would have that. Maybe I'd marry a prince. Everything would be taken care of.

"But now I am convinced that shallow, artificial happiness is not the answer, either. You can get that from drugs. If everyone settled for that estate, the world would shortly come to an end."

John considered that. Betsy was a pretty smart girl. She refused to accept the easy answers. She knew she wanted happiness, but she was choosy how she got it. Here was something he could comment on. It tied in, not too remotely, with his own problem: that of the inconsistencies in his surroundings. In fact, what he had here *was* a kind of make-believe happiness that he found empty in practice. He didn't want satisfaction in ignorance. He wanted to know the truth. It might be ugly; it might even hurt him, but. . . .

"Supper, John," Mom called.

The important chain of thought had been broken again! He grasped at the last link, determined to have the meaning. The truth might be ugly, painful, but it would be *real*. Not a cardboard. . . .

"John?"

"Coming, Mom!"

Talk of three wishes! He wished he had a decent chance to *think*! Morosely, he went downstairs.

2

*Outside
the Zoo*

After supper John washed the dishes. This was not a chore he had to do. He had volunteered one evening, surprising and pleasing Mom. Then, ashamed to confess that he had only needed a pretext to postpone particularly dull homework, he had stayed with it, night after night. This time it provided him with another mindless exercise while he thought things out.

He had been pondering things he couldn't explain. Betsy had written of the fallacy of artificial happiness. The two jibed, almost. He had drawn a mental parallel between them, made them add up to something significant . . . almost.

Something was wrong. He had to find a situation that accounted for a cat with a prehensile tail, a tree-climbing dog, and the strange restrictions on his freedom.

Betsy's letter-essay suggested that the best wish of all was for information. Well, it didn't say so in so many words, but it seemed to be leading up to that. To know, or to have the means to discover, the truth, whatever it might be. And if the truth made the knower miserable, that was still better than contented ignorance.

He agreed with her. He didn't exactly *like* her, but he realized that she could be a valuable ally. By pooling their two sets of information they might indeed come at the truth. Maybe that was why they weren't allowed to meet yet. They might compare notes and discover something vital. If their letters were censored . . . well, it might be possible to get around that.

He finished the dishes and called Canute for the evening walk. He still needed thinking time. The only way he could communicate with Betsy was by letter, censored or not. He could not just put his suspicions into writing, so what could he do?

Canute stopped to sniff at a tree. John was momentarily tempted to tell the dog to climb it, but he suppressed the urge. He was lucky the hidden watchers—the ones that he had long ago invented as a game but now firmly believed in—hadn't been alert during that first climb. *If* they had missed it; if not, the dog might be gone in the morning, like the kitten. . . . No! He wouldn't let anyone take Canute! He would be alert and stop them somehow, even if he had to fight in the night!

He needed more information before deciding anything. Betsy might help. If he could just write to her privately. . . .

A code! One she would comprehend, but not the censor. It would have to be a very simple code, and that increased the risk. He couldn't work it out on paper in advance, either, because a watcher might see his notes. That made it a real challenge. Every tenth word? She would never pick that up unless she were looking for just that type of thing. Forlorn hope. First word in each sentence? Maybe, but still pretty clumsy. Either way he'd have to write a long, wordy letter to put across a short message—a message that would probably be wasted.

If he could only give her some hint—but the censor would pick it up, too! He was still stuck.

And when he came down to it, how could he be sure that Betsy herself was real? He had never met her. All he knew of her was her letters and her picture. Obviously *somebody* wrote the one and posed for the other, but that was hardly proof that Betsy-as-he-knew-her existed. Maybe his correspondent *was* the censor!

But again: If Betsy were *not* real, why should they have taken all the trouble to invent her? He hadn't wanted to correspond. There were girls in school, some fairly attractive, even if their skins weren't real. There was no point in signing him up with a stranger, particularly not another imitation.

He had picked up a useful rule of thumb from his readings: Accept the simplest explanation he could find—for anything. He chuckled. By that token his whole project was useless! The simplest explanation for Betsy was that his folks thought she was a better match for him than any of the local girls, but she lived too far away for immediate visits. For Canute's climbing, the simplest explanation was that dogs *could* climb trees, and the encyclopedia hadn't thought this needed mentioning. For the kitten. . . .

The kitten was harder, because cats were *not* supposed to have prehensile tails, and his folks *had* been upset when he mentioned it (upset but not surprised?!), and the cat *had* disappeared. It was pushing coincidence to dismiss the connection. It was as though the cat had not been a cat at all, and once he was on the verge of discovering that. . . .

He felt the chill across his shoulders, up his neck. *Not a real cat!* Talk of simple explanations!

Maybe Canute was not a real dog, either. And the kids at school were not real kids. And his folks not real parents. Maybe the whole town of Newton. . . . But this line of thinking didn't seem to lead to any answers.

He would query Betsy. Two heads were better than one. She might not answer, or she might not exist as a person, but the effort wouldn't cost him much, and it might bring out something important.

Canute was sniffing his way back toward the house. John had to set up his message and his code before he got there so that he could type without seeming to make much of it.

Let's see . . . something simple and direct for the message. "Let's compare notes. Something is wrong. Does your dog climb trees?" But she didn't have a dog. She had a bird. Great show! All right: "Have you ever been out of town?" Not good, but he was pressed for time. Now how to encode it. Why not every third word? That wouldn't be too complicated to figure out. With an opening hint: "Sometimes I think we'd learn more just by reading every third word." Yes, that was good. He was at the doorstep. He'd have to work out the rest extemporaneously.

In his room he began the letter:

"Dear Betsy, I've been thinking about your recent comments but must admit they confuse me. Sometimes I think we'd do better just reading every third word. I mean, let's start to compare some such notes. I think something might develop. Is there any wrong or right—does any of your—" Oops! He had started on the dog query instead of the out-of-town query. And the letter wasn't too bright, generally. This was harder to fit together than he had thought. His third words, after the key sentence, were okay: "let's . . . compare . . . notes . . . something . . . is . . . wrong . . . does . . . your"—but the overall text was ridiculously clumsy. Well, he was stuck with it now.

". . . does any of your thinking." Stuck again. How could he fit in "dog" without being too obvious. And he didn't even want to ask her about her nonexistent dog! He kept confusing himself, trying to concentrate on three things at once.

He could write a horrible letter, then make a show of rereading it and tearing it up in disgust. If he had to. That might fool the watchers.

". . . does any of your thinking fly bird or moth like out the strange cage of stuff?" Ugh! This was getting ridiculous. He had to stop.

"Sorry," he typed. "I can't seem to organize my thoughts tonight. Maybe you get the idea." Up to "does . . . your . . . bird . . . like . . . strange . . . stuff?" anyway. That would have to do.

He filled out the letter with routine chaff: how he looked forward to meeting her, the recent weather, etc. He had pretty well mangled his code letter; it wasn't as good an idea as it had seemed at first, but he was too stubborn to give it up now. He addressed the envelope, sealed it, stuck on a postage stamp, and put it in the box at the front door for the mailman to pick up next day. At least that took care of his weekly missive!

Betsy's reply, a few days later, amazed him. She had picked up the gambit and replied in kind. Her message, spaced every third word far more skillfully than his own blundering effort, was this:

"I have known for some time that it wasn't real. All the pets are alien creatures. You and I are zoo specimens, due to be mated next year so as to preserve the species in captivity. I tried to break out last year, so they watch me closely now. I will help you escape if you agree to rescue me in return."

John pondered the letter, so innocent on the surface, so forceful in code. Was she pulling his leg? He hadn't really *believed* this watchers business, had he? Was she laughing her head off over his gullibility?

Maybe—but somehow he didn't think so. Her bluff was too easily called, and what she said jibed too nicely with his own observations. All he had asked her was whether her bird acted strangely; he had not mentioned his suspicion that everything else, including the people, was a mock-up. And if Betsy were the censor, she certainly wouldn't encourage his suspicions!

She must be like him, with similar experiences and suspicions. Now she proposed to bargain with him, and why not? But there was one more check he had to make before he committed himself.

That night he did something he had not done in years: He sneaked out. He simply waited until the household was asleep, then got up and walked out the front door. He didn't think about the watchers.

He heard a noise just as he was closing the door. Canute had heard him and wanted to come along. If he shut the door, the dog would scratch at it and howl, alerting everybody. He had either to let Canute join him or to give up the venture. Also, he suddenly realized that he dared not leave the dog alone, tonight or any night. That would be the moment Canute disappeared. . . .

"Quiet!" he whispered, opening the door and feeling a marked relief. However alien the dog might be in reality, he was comforting to have along. There was no question about Canute's personal loyalty. Together they faced the cool, still, dark outside.

They walked toward the township limit. John used his flashlight once he was clear of the house. He had never been beyond the Newton line, but tonight it would be different. Something had always happened to stop him before—the road would be temporarily blocked, or a severe storm would come up, or he would meet someone going the other way and be distracted. He had been frustrated but not suspicious—until now.

Betsy claimed they were both zoo specimens. Well, modern zoos put their animals in superficially compatible habitats so that the stupid ones might not even be aware of their confinement. They were supposed to be happier and healthier that way and would breed in captivity. Rage surged through him. Not *this* animal!

Canute woofed, thinking John's reaction meant danger. John reached down to pat the speckled shoulder reassuringly. If Newton were a zoo, Canute was still a friend!

This was too slow. John switched off the flashlight and let his eyes adapt to the night. There was some moonglow, hazed by clouds. "Lead the way, Canute!" he whispered, beginning to run. "To the fence!"

Canute led. He had done this before, picking out the best trail. John followed with confidence, knowing the dog would not betray him into any rut or bush. The strikingly marked fur was easy to see, in contrast to the ground. He judged they were making ten or twelve miles an hour before he got winded and had to take a walk-break.

In half an hour they reached the fence that marked the town limit. It was not an auspicious barrier—just a four-foot-high wire mesh with a double strand of barbed wire along the top. To keep the cows clear, he had been told. He paced along it, pretty sure the fence was bugged. If he touched it anywhere, someone would come. It would seem accidental, but his exploration would be halted. He was sure of that. He had to get through without any contact.

He used his flash, casting about in the growing-up pasture here. He might construct a stile, but that would take time, and he didn't have a hatchet or any cord or hammer or nails, and he couldn't afford the noise even if he knew how to assemble it, and he would have real trouble in the dark. He had to get over that fence in a hurry.

He walked farther, frustrated. Such simple things were balking him! The flash splashed against a rock. There was an old stone wall, falling apart. These massive but ineffective barriers had been used, he understood, to fence in sheep, maybe a century ago. Pretty dumb animal to be restrained by no more than this. Anybody could climb over! Just how stupid did the keepers figure John Smith was?

He realized that he had come to accept Betsy's theory, even though he had not verified it yet. Anyway, here was his stile: He could build a rampart of rocks.

Half an hour later he was dirty and tired, but he had a crude pyramid as high as the fence. He could jump over easily from its top, and so could Canute. Coming back would be more of a problem, but that was the least of his worries at the moment.

He flung himself over, landing hard and rolling before he could get righted. "Come, Canute!" he called softly. The dog leaped down with surprising finesse.

They were outside the township of Newton—the presumed limit of his prison. But John couldn't detect any difference. He let Canute lead the way through the semidarkness, away from the fence. He felt let down. He had been keyed up for something spectacular, or at least a change. If there were nothing but empty countryside. . . .

There *had* to be something else! Dad had to go somewhere when he drove off for work. The truck supplying the local stores had to come from somewhere. Newton could not exist in a vacuum. It didn't matter whether it was a legitimate town or a zoo; there was a framework of some kind.

Assured, he moved on, running, walking, running, following Canute. The forest continued while his nervousness increased. *Had* he imagined it all, and was he now trekking through perfectly innocent, ordinary countryside, making a fool of himself?

After twenty minutes he saw a light. His heart pounded, and not just from the running. Now he would find out! He warned the dog to silence and approached, ducking behind trees and bushes. It was a house of sorts. Not like any in Newton. This one was half-round, like a soap bubble on water, and it shimmered: a glowing twenty-foot hemisphere with boxes stuck to it.

As he crept closer, he discerned more detail. The house was not bubble-shaped after all—it was octagonal. Its main diameter was about twelve feet, and the four cubes bracing it were about five feet on a side. The cubes were opaque, but the walls between them were transparent. He was sure it was a house because he could see people inside.

They were brown people. A brown girl slept on a cushion against one outer panel, her hand touching the glass. A brown man, probably her father, sat poring over something on a table. John didn't see any others, but they could be hidden in the cubicles.

Brown people. If all the artificial skin were peeled away from the people of Newton, they might be like this. Betsy's statement had been confirmed. Or had it? This was not like any zoo he had heard of!

More important: this house. It was futuristic. He could tell without further investigation that it beat anything of 1960 by a century of progress, at least.

It hung in the air a yard above the ground, but nothing held it there. It had internal illumination, but there were no power wires leading to it. It was tiny, but the evident comfort of its visible occupants proved that it wasn't stuffy. John saw no kitchen or closets or sanitary facilities—and if those things all fit in the cubicles, they had to be mighty efficient. This wasn't any setup for his benefit. He had come in secret and struck it randomly, following Canute's nose. Most likely it was typical of the dwellings outside of Newton.

Brown people in a house of the future. What an item! It was exciting, and more than enough to think about. Time for him to get home. He would just about have time to straddle the fence—he realized belatedly he could prepare a pole to vault over—and lift Canute past, dismantle his unwieldy rampart, and get into bed before morning. He didn't want to get caught outside the zoo the way Betsy had been and have his freedom restricted more stringently.

And he'd better agree to her terms! Now he was sure he didn't want to stay in staid Newton, when the future lay outside. Literally.

3

A Strange Mistake

The better part of a year passed. John graduated from high school and dutifully wrote his weekly letters to Betsy, making sure they were dull. He whistled as he performed household chores and did not ask awkward questions. He took up gymnastics, becoming quite proficient at running and jumping, and he trained Canute to do some remarkable tricks. Mom and Dad were very pleased.

Those dull letters exchanged with Betsy, however, were in increasingly sophisticated code, and some of Canute's tricks were meaningless within the Newton existence. And occasionally John applied brown makeup and hurdled the fence and explored the surrounding region. He raided an unoccupied floating house and learned by trial, error, and more error how to handle modern facilities, including the fantastic communicator. His grades in the Newton school were indifferent, but had he been graded on the total amount he learned in that year, he would have been the township champion.

The date outside was 2375, and the planet was "Standard." John was apparently the last healthy, sane, young, purebred Caucasian human male in existence, and Betsy was the last healthy, etc., female. They were to be mated so that this unique line could be continued. The rest of humanity was Standard: an evenly melted mixture of the assorted human stocks of the planet earth.

Neither John nor Betsy could ascertain why this time and place in history had been chosen for this oasis of the past. Was there some prejudice against the purebred Caucasian stock, and had these two white subjects been kept in seclusion and ignorance so that they would not be ravaged by the horrors of their ancestry? If so, what had happened to the world they thought they knew?

Yet if the Caucasian heritage was so evil, why had they been kept alive at all, let alone in such an elaborate setting? The zoos were a good deal more elegant than seemed necessary. But a zoo, whether as fancy as a palace or simple as a manacle on the ankle, was still a zoo. Two things John and Betsy agreed on: to thwart this mechanically calculated mating plan and to learn the truth about the vanished white race. They worked out their escape, refining the details week after week. Once they

were free and safe, and once they knew the full
story, they would go their separate ways.

Then, only two weeks before they were scheduled to meet, Betsy wrote in code: "There is a third
zoo." That was all she knew. Her father had a wrist
TV disguised as an old-time watch. He had forgotten it one night after removing it for a shower, and
she had sneaked into his room and watched it for
half an hour. The picture was three-dimensional,
even though barely an inch across; she had had to
put her eye up close to make out the detail, and it
was like looking through a telescope. She saw
routine news and a weather report, and they had
flashed maps of the continent to mark the scheduled
rain regions. Population densities and similar factors were overlaid in color, but she hadn't had time
to analyze them. She spotted her own area, and it
was blank. So was John's Newton. And one more.

They had no time to hash it out thoroughly. She
might have misread the maps or misinterpreted the
coding of the overlays. Even if she were correct,
there could be a separate explanation for the third
blank—a supply depot, perhaps. But they could not
dismiss the possibility that they were not quite
alone. They agreed to modify their program accordingly. They would somehow check out the third
zoo before they split.

John spent his last night in Newton quietly. He
wondered if his parents—actually two bleached-
white Standards assigned to this task—suspected

that he planned to leave the zoo forever tomorrow. Of course, Mom and Dad were good people, even if they lived a lie. They were dedicated. The other inhabitants of the Newton zoo could peel and scrub and resume their natural skin color and their normal existence each evening, but Mom and Dad had to maintain their roles constantly. They had done everything they were supposed to and never once let on that it was only a job. It was not their fault that he had seen through the masquerade that day when he had jokingly ordered Canute to climb the tree, and the dog had not been smart enough to reject the directive.

Did Mom and Dad approve of what they were doing? He doubted it. If there had been a certain coldness, it had not been directed at him. Things had always been harmonious but not that close; though he certainly bore them no enmity, he was not strongly attached. Would they be punished for letting him escape? The question struck him with greater misgiving than seemed warranted, and he was surprised to find his eyes moist. He was suddenly aware that Mom and Dad were more important to him than he had realized. They must love him a little, just as he loved Canute, and the feeling was reciprocal. It did not matter, on the personal level, that they were not his true parents and Canute not a true dog. The relationships were more binding than the facts.

He would have to leave a note to exonerate them. He went to the typewriter, then caught himself and passed by it to the closet, pretending to check his suit for the forthcoming occasion. The watchers could be watching. If he made a note, someone would see it too soon, and the whole thing would be ruined. Twenty-fourth-century technology could keep him under perpetual observation without any direct "bugs," he was quite certain now. His nocturnal excursions had escaped notice only because there had seemed to be no reason to watch him sleeping every night. He had kept them to a minimum, though, refusing to push his luck unnecessarily.

Mom and Dad would just have to take their chances. He regretted it, but there was no other way.

The telephone rang. Mom pounced on it immediately, though she had never been the nervous type. "Hello," she said and listened for a moment. "Where?" Another pause, then: "Thank you," gravely.

"She's come," Dad said, touching his little moustache, and Mom nodded. Oddly, they both seemed as much on edge as John himself.

"At the bus station," Mom said. "She—she's alone."

'I'll go pick her up," John volunteered, knowing that this was what they wanted. Some kind of mistake had been made in the delivery, and they were embarrassed and nonplussed.

Betsy was supposed to arrive on the train with a

chaperon. That way the Standards would be sure she remained under control and that nothing was given away. But she had turned up on the bus and alone. Had she thumbed her nose at the system by giving her chaperon the slip? No wonder Mom and Dad were covertly shaking! What if she had escaped entirely? They wanted time to recover from the shock—and to bawl out someone on the phone.

John rode his bicycle, though he realized that this would not do to bring her back. Well, the two of them could walk—and anyway, he would not bring her to the house.

This confusion of arrival actually played into his hands. He would need no ruse to get out from under the supervision of the elders. He and Betsy could put their escape plan into effect at once. But he was upset, too. What fool stunt had Betsy pulled? Their plan required everything to be absolutely routine until it was time for the big break; it was important that the Standards have no hint of what was planned. Betsy's rash behavior could have alerted the watchers and destroyed any chance to flee!

He pedaled faster, knowing that he was over-reacting. Once more he felt remorse at what this would do to his folks—and hers. They were imitation parents, but they were good, kind people. But it had to be done (if it could be done!) if he and Betsy were not to be lifelong zoo specimens.

The bus station was hardly more than a notch in the wall behind the five-and-dime store. There were only two buses a day—one on Sundays—and they seldom had more than one or two passengers. The driver sold the tickets; there was no proper office. It was just a partial shelter against rain or sun and an uncomfortable place to wait. Betsy would not be pleased.

He wheeled around the corner of Main and Third, making the one-block jog north to Birch, where the bus alley diverged. It was dark here, after the bright sunshine, but he followed Canute's white network confidently. In a moment the bus shelter loomed, and he saw a dark figure standing against the wall. Canute woofed.

John's eyes were adjusting to the shadow. At first he saw little more than a white robe. Then he made out tremendous yellow ear pendants, each like a quarter slice of honeydew melon. Then he lost control of the bicycle and crashed ignominiously to the pavement.

"Humé?" she called.

John fought back the pain of a skinned knee as he extricated himself from the wreckage. "Betsy?"

It could hardly be Betsy. This was a deeply brown-skinned girl—black, really—as far from Standard tan as he was. She wore a floor-length robe, scarf-tied hair, and huge earrings. She came to stand beside him solicitously, her dark hands clasping each other.

John straightened. "Is that—are those real gold?" he asked her, his eyes compelled by the yellow. Each pendant was a good six inches long.

"Yes," she said, as though that were obvious. "You are not Humé."

"I'm John. And you're not Betsy."

"I am Ala." She also had a delicate gold ring set in her nose, and a thin black braid of hair dropped across her forehead.

They looked at each other, a white boy and a black girl. "I think there has been a mistake," John said at last, "and not just a little one."

"You were to take a foreign bride? An Arab?"

"An *Arab*? No, an American."

"I was sent to Humé of Bornu." She made a face. "*Bornu!*"

"Very bad," he agreed diplomatically, not knowing where Bornu was supposed to be. "Look—something is wrong, but we can't talk here. Someone might—overhear." Already he was certain that quick privacy was crucial. This opened up a whole new dimension to the zoo-escape problem!

She looked at him more thoroughly, and he was impressed by her bearing. She was just about his own age and very pretty. "You are not of Bornu or anywhere in the Sudan, yet—" Here she stopped abruptly.

"Yet not Standard?" he asked softly.

She seemed not to hear him. She looked down, her great golden earrings shifting forward. "You have a beautiful dog."

Canute's ears perked. He moved up to sniff her hand, tail half-wagging.

"Walk beside me," John said. "We'll try to bluff it through. Don't look at any other people."

They moved at a moderate pace out of the bus

alley and northward along Third Street, ignoring the townspeople they passed, and the natives of Newton ignored them, though he knew there would be amazed discussion afterward. By acting boldly he hoped to carry it off, to make it seem as though he were *supposed* to be walking with a black girl.

Third terminated in a parklike dead end. They bypassed the barrier and advanced into open country. Once among the trees, they changed direction and began a wide arc westward.

"We can be seen here, but not heard, I think," John said at last. "I've checked out the region as well as I could."

"They cannot hear us from the city unless we shout," she said. "Please tell me now. Where is this remarkable place, and who are you? I have never been told of a city like this, and the people are all jinn-white."

"They aren't really white. They're Standards— brown people with white covering. Halfway between you and me."

"Tauregs?"

"Standards. People of the twenty-fourth century."

She turned her head with the glow of gold to stare at him in amazement. "What do you mean, John of the strange city?"

Suddenly he realized that she didn't know about the Standards. He had assumed from her reactions that she did, but now he saw that he had misinterpreted them. She thought all this was real!

This development complicated things even more. Obviously Ala was from that third zoo, sent to him by mistake. What a blunder! But at any time the Standard authorities would untangle their mix-up and act to correct it. Whatever he had to say to this girl he would have to say quickly—and she had no idea of the situation! Yet she was a potential ally. He might never have a chance to talk with another purebred specimen, other than Betsy. This was his opportunity to establish a rapport between zoos— one that might help to free them all. He had to take advantage of this incredible break. He had to get through to her!

Something nagged the back of his mind but wouldn't jell. Be methodical, he told himself. Haste makes waste, or whatever. Do this properly, avoid further confusion, save crucial time.

"What is the date? The year?" he asked her. Once that common ground had been established, he could show her how it failed to jibe with other facts.

"The twentieth day of Zu'lkadah, nine hundred seventy-six," she said.

"Nineteen seventy-six! That's fifteen years ahead of me!" he exclaimed. It had not occurred to him that his date might fail to match hers! It was the world of the Standards he expected to differ from the world of the purebreds.

"Nine hundred seventy-six," she said clearly. "Are you mocking me with your talk of a thousand years hence?"

John hesitated, appalled at the time chasm that he

suddenly found between them. A thousand years!
How could he discuss twenty-fourth-century concepts—or even the twentieth century's—with this
girl from the Dark Ages? But he had to try, for he
might have no more than a thousand seconds to
make intellectual contact. "That month—
Zulwhatchims. . . ."

"Zu'lkadah. Next month I take the hajj,
bareheaded and wearing just two pieces of cloth, as
prescribed," Ala answered.

"Where—where do you live?"

"Mopti. But after the hajj I will go to Jenne, to
the university."

University—it was the lone familiar term in a
linguistic morass. "Mopti? Is that a city? In what
state, what country?"

She glanced at him as though he were babbling.
"In the lakes region, of course. On the Niger, in
Songhai."

He caught hold of another word. "The Niger?
Isn't that a river in Africa?"

Again that perplexed glance. "Yes, of course.
Songhai is the greatest empire in Africa, and the
richest under Allah. Surely you know that?"

Allah! "You're not Christian?"

"An infidel? You *are* mocking me!" She was
angry now, and prettily so. "Tribal gods are one
thing, but—" She stopped walking and faced
about, her ear decorations swinging out grandly. "I
should not have walked with you. I must go back
and find out what happened to the proper caravan. I

was to travel to Bornu, to Kanem, to see Humé. How I came to this heathen place I cannot say. I supposed you were a Peul slave messenger, or even a bonded Moroccan, because of your strange pallor. I see now that you are no honest tribesman of Africa, but a foreigner, perhaps even a Portuguese slaver. I will not soil my hands on you." She concluded her speech and started back toward the town.

John dived to block her path. "Ala, I'm not mocking you! I'm trying to—look, I'm a white-skinned Christian American who lives almost a thousand years after you. Supposedly. You can see I'm different and my whole town is different. *How is it possible that we two are together now?*"

She was silent for a moment, and he hoped she was realizing that on the face of it their meeting was impossible in the real world. Once she saw that, she would be ready to listen to his explanation and to verify it for herself.

"I see you are different," she said at last. "I do not see you living a thousand years hence. Let me go."

He had not been touching her, but now he put his hand on her arm just below the white sleeve. He felt the immediate tension of her small, firm muscle. "I'm *not* living a thousand years later! That's the point. We can't coexist in the—the framework the Standards have given us—so we're actually——"

"The palm leaf despises the hippo," she said.

Amazed, John let his hand drop. She brushed by

him, walking swiftly away. John was jolted back to action. It was as though her mysterious remark had cast a spell over him, momentarily—but he couldn't let her go. Not yet.

Again he got in front of her and barred the way. "Haven't you seen the Standards? Tan people, under that white-painted surface, that shellac. Under the black, for you, I guess. They control us. They——"

"The palm leaf despises the hippo," she repeated, staring regally past him.

"Oh, dry up!" he exclaimed. "I'm trying to help you!"

She looked uncertain. "Dry it?"

"Dry your damn palm leaf! Bake it under the sun all day, for all I care! If you won't listen, you won't listen."

He stood aside, but she did not move. "I will listen, John," she said softly, and she almost smiled.

John swallowed his anger and amazement and plunged in. "You are a purebred African. I am a purebred American. You were raised in an African village. I was raised in an American village. But you never saw any other villages, did you, and neither did I." He paused to take a breath, watching her face for reaction. He was guessing about her background, but her failure to object confirmed his belief. She *had* been raised in a zoo.

"You never saw those other villages because there *were* none," he continued. "They taught you geography, but it was all in texts, or whatever you use in Songhai. You never actually went anywhere. When you wanted to go, they made excuses, but they never let you out. They told you you would travel when you got older, or when you finished your education, or when you married. Always sometime in the future. They kept you close because they *couldn't* show you any real places."

She nodded slowly, her massive earrings flashing in the sunlight once more.

"And then they sent you to the man they had selected for you—Humé. Only someone slipped up, and you arrived at the American exhibit, and probably"—he paused, just now making the connection—"probably right now Humé is talking with Betsy. The white girl. Because we are the only purebreds in the world, and it's *not* earth. It's another planet, and everyone else is of mixed race. The people you know in your village—scratch their arms, and there's brown skin underneath, much lighter than yours. You've seen that, haven't you?"

"Yes," she murmured.

"And there are no animals. Except pets. You know what a dog is?" But of course she did; she had complimented Canute. When she nodded, he continued: "You know what a dog can do—and what it *can't* do?"

She nodded again.

"Well, watch this. Canute!"

Canute, sniffing around some large roots, lifted his head and bounded over with his tail wagging

briskly. He was well over fifty pounds now—a lot
of dog. John pointed to the nearest tree. "Climb!"

The dog hesitated, then climbed.

"Well, that's my case," John said. "We're all
zoo specimens. If we continue the way the Standards—the brown-skinned people—want us to,
we'll make fine exhibits. And maybe if we purebreds have children of our own someday, the Standards will take them away to be raised in other
exhibits, just as we have been raised. Must be
pretty interesting, watching a freak person in his
natural habitat. A real moneymaker."

"They don't use money," Ala said.

"You know what I mean. They can see us
somehow, all the time. They—" He stopped,
realizing what she had said. "You knew! You know
about the Standards!"

"Who did you think spoke to your keepers?"

"Who—" He had a moment's confusion.
"That's it! That was what was nagging me! That
phone call saying you were at the bus station! You
couldn't have done that unless——"

"I had the coachman do it," she admitted. "I did
not know how to use your speaking tube. 'Inform
the man I'm here,' I said, and so he spoke and then
went away in his hollow dragon. He was a
Standard."

A white-painted Standard or a black-painted
Standard? he wondered, but decided not to get
entangled in such details now. "Why didn't you just
tell me at once, if you knew?"

"I did not trust you. Your aspect is alarmingly pale, you know."

John was furious. "All this time you made me waste! They'll discover their mistake anytime."

She shrugged. "If Allah wills. What can we do, John?"

"We can escape! Betsy and I have—but why should I trust you, either?"

She faced about again and resumed walking in their original direction as though nothing were wrong. John, ashamed of his outburst, had to fall in beside her. "I give you my secret: three numbers," she said, looking straight ahead.

"Look, I'm sorry I. . . ."

"Can you remember them?"

So she wouldn't let him apologize! "Numbers! What good are they?"

"They are called coordinates." That word was obviously alien to her. "Of my village and two others. When you escape, seek them out. That is all I can do for you; I know no more."

Coordinates of other zoos! This was invaluable information. "I'm sorry," he said urgently. "You were right to be cautious. Let me write down your figures."

"No. They can see us. They could read your paper. You must remember the numbers, as I do."

He nodded soberly. "I'll memorize them."

"0544071364," she said. "377——"

"Hey! I can't remember all that!"

"You must. 3777767256. 0000150055. Those are the three. Mine is the third."

"But those aren't coordinates! They're just numbers! I can't make head or tail of them!"

"Where I live it is hot," she said. "Palm trees, elephants—we *do* have an elephant——"

"What's that got to do with—" Then he made the connection. "You must live near the equator. And your number is full of zeroes. Maybe. . . ."

"Do you remember them all now?"

"No. Give me the first slowly. I'll try to fix it in my mind. Then the other two. I'll figure out what they mean later."

She repeated the numbers, and he concentrated as though cramming for the years's most important exam—as perhaps he was. The second figure was easier because of the row of sevens, and the third was no trouble at all. Maybe he was getting the hang of it. "I think I have them," he said at last and hoped it was true.

By then they had circled to the main road. "It goes nowhere," John said. "I followed it one night. Runs into a forest and peters out into nothing. Yet Dad drives to work that way every morning."

"Drives to work?"

"Oops—you didn't have cars in nine hundred seventy-six! It—it's like riding an elephant, only it's metal. A metal elephant you sit inside."

She laughed. "The Standards don't use metal elephants, either."

"No. They have floating balls. But what did you make of the bus, if you don't know about driving?"

"Bus?"

"You were at the bus station. You must've come in a bus, and you saw the driver drive away."

"Oh, you mean the hollow dragon!" she considered. "I left on the elephant. Then"—she faltered—"I must have slept."

"So you don't really know how you got here? It figures."

"Perhaps on one of their floating balls."

"Probably. I have an identity key that will make one of them operate for me. If you ever see one of those balls coming down on your village, get over to it quickly; it'll mean I've escaped and figured out your location. I'm not fooling—the Standards never fly those balls in sight of a zoo." Then he had a disturbing second thought. "You *do* want to escape?"

"I want to take my hajj, John, my pilgrimage to Mecca, next month."

"Oh, sure. After that, I mean. And your—you know—Humé?"

"I do not know Humé," she said disdainfully. "But I may not be at my village. The university of Jenne. . . ."

She was avoiding his question, refusing to commit herself, but she *had* given him the coordinates. "I may come anyway. If this foul-up that introduced us doesn't change everything."

"I'm glad it happened," Ala said.

John looked at her, surprised and gratified. "Yes! So am I."

They were in sight of Newton now, but it didn't matter.

4

Escape from Newton

Mom was gently shaking him awake. "John, it's breakfast time, and you aren't up yet! The eggs will get cold."

He sat up dazedly. *What had happened?*

Mom was watching him with concern. "Do you feel all right, dear? You were talking in your sleep."

John rubbed his eyes. Canute was there, tail wagging. Everything was in order except his own head. The dizziness passed reluctantly, and chaotic images danced behind his eyeballs. "Guess I was dreaming, Mom," and for a moment he believed it. Then he caught himself repeating "0544071364" and knew that the black girl with the golden ornaments had been no fantasy. Somehow the Standards had erased that day and started over!

He must have been drugged. That would account for his unusual confusion upon waking and the fleeting nightmare visions. He usually woke clearheaded.

John played along. The ruse might have worked if he had not long since known about the Standards. He would have shaken off the memory of Ala, her Moslem religion, her thousand-year antiquity, along with the irrelevant notions. She would, indeed, have become a dream. But he *did* know about the Standards, and so did she. And now he had another major piece of the puzzle. Black purebreds as well as white purebreds! Each one in his or her own zoo. . . .

One other thing: The Standards certainly could not have overheard yesterday's conversation, or they would have known that he knew about them and was plotting to escape. And they would never have tried this simplistic stunt or given him his chance to join with Betsy! So he had been right: They could see but not hear outside the developed town. That was good to verify, and it gave him renewed confidence.

But he could do nothing at the moment. If he gave himself away, it could lead to trouble for all the purebreds—himself and Betsy, Ala and Humé. He had to act natural now. Once he was free—if he got free, if his plan with Betsy worked. . . .

He snapped his fingers as he trotted down the stairs. He *could* do something now! He could figure out that coordinates system so he would know exactly where to find Ala! But he was unable to concentrate, for Mom and Dad kept him occupied with one preparatory chore or another all morning.

This time they took no chances. Betsy arrived in an automobile with her folks. John could tell at a glance that she was real, whereas her parents were painted Standards like his own. There were many telltale traces apart from the skin, once he knew what to look for. The contour of the head was subtly different, the spacing of the features, the shape of the nose, the thickness of lips and brows—the Standards were certainly of a distinct race, regardless of their color.

"Come, John; mustn't be bashful," Dad said with forced heartiness.

"I'm not," John said, doing his best to *look* bashful. Who was fooling whom, after yesterday's episode?

The older folks got out on either side of the car and came forward to shake hands with Mom and Dad. John hardly looked at them; his attention was on Betsy—as it was supposed to be, but not for the reason the elders thought.

Betsy bore a certain resemblance to her picture, but the portrait had obviously been retouched, and she was older now, seventeen. He was sure she saw him the same way. For a moment he had a really uncomfortable doubt: Would this carefully nurtured girl actually risk a safe, easy life to become a fugitive with him? Could he trust her?

"How do you do?" Betsy said, startling him into a foolish smile.

John held out his hand, changed his mind, then reversed again and shook hands clumsily. "Uh, fine, how are you?" This was unexpectedly awkward, and he was, after all, bashful. He had made plans—*they* had made plans—with cool assurance. Now it all seemed ridiculous.

The four parents were beaming. Now John felt guilty, too. It was all so realistic, and he was sure these particular Standards meant well, by their own definitions. What he contemplated was a tremendous betrayal to people who had invested at least fifteen years of their lives in this. . . .

"Why don't you show me around, John?" Betsy hinted softly.

He nodded dumbly, furious with her for nudging him like that and with himself for losing his grip. Yesterday he had been in command! (*Was* it a dream, then?) She took his arm, and he realized he should have proffered it. They walked away from the house. He felt those eight parental eyes on his back. What a freeze artist he turned out to be in the crunch! If Betsy hadn't taken over, they'd still be standing beside the car trying to think of something worth saying.

He and Betsy were together now. They had been building up to this moment for a year, both openly and in code. The program of the Standards had them visiting together for a week, then separating for a month before meeting again in college: to make sure the specimens were compatible, he thought angrily.

The code plan was for them to take an innocent preliminary walk, evincing proper adolescent shyness, and vault the Newton township fence in a sudden coordinated action. Properly executed, this would catch the secret observers by surprise and make time to set up the second phase.

"Down there is Newton," he said.

"The town," she said solemnly. "How nice."

He felt the heat in his face. *Sarcastic minx!*

Canute pushed against the front door and bounded after them, tail wagging. He caught up to them and frisked about, his paws scattering pebbles in his eagerness.

"Get away!" Betsy exclaimed as the dog nosed her dress. "Get away from me, you dirty animal!"

"That's Canute," John said, irritated at her attitude. "He always comes along."

"He always comes along," she mimicked, brushing a smudge of dirt from her shoe.

Canute, sensing her hostility, became chastened. He dog-trotted on the side away from her, tail near his legs. John was furious.

They got away from the adults and passed the copse of spruce trees. "You knew about Canute!" he said in a low, terse voice. "I've trained him——"

"We can't take a *dog*!" she whispered back. "You never said he'd—come along." She meant along on the escape but of course could not refer to that openly.

"Well, he's coming," John said with determination.

"Well, he's coming!" she mimicked again.

John was so angry he could not talk. He had had no idea a girl could be this obnoxious. It hadn't shown in her letters at all.

They cut through a section of the copse, then across the pasture toward the town limit, seemingly aimlessly. Perhaps it *was* aimless, he thought miserably. If Betsy was this difficult already, what would she be like when the going got rough? He might be better off to make the break alone. Except that he had promised, and he couldn't risk leaving her behind to give away all their secrets.

Two things were certain: He was not going to stay in the zoo, and he wasn't going to desert Canute.

"This is the township line," he said aloud. "Up farther there's a path back toward Newton. We can go back that way." He suspected that the supervisors could see and hear in the vicinity of the fence, by day at least, and this would put them off guard. They would figure they could relax for ten or fifteen minutes. That was part of the plan.

Halfway to the path he detoured silently into a patch of forest while Betsy walked straight ahead, chatting innocently about the weather. He brought out two poles. He handed one to her. If she were serious, this was the crisis point. If not. . . .

Without waiting he ran at the fence, jammed his pole into the ground, and vaulted neatly over. He could have hurdled it without a pole, since he had practiced high jumping in the past year, but this was safer. He landed, kept his feet, and ran for the cover of a tree.

". . . but I do admit it's cooler under the trees, here," Betsy was saying, but she was running as he looked back. "Shade and a little breeze, and who needs air conditioning?" She vaulted over as easily as he, her dress spreading out like a parachute as she dropped. Her pole fell next to his on the inside. In a moment she joined him at the tree.

"Watch," he whispered, not certain whether he was pleased or frustrated at the certainty of her commitment. She was smart and athletic, obviously, but her personality. . . .

Canute came up and caught the first pole in his teeth, dragging it away from the fence. He tugged it back into the forest, out of sight. Then he returned for the second. John didn't say anything. He was sure this had made his point: Canute's presence was justified. It had never occured to him before that she might challenge the dog's right to make the escape with them.

Canute emerged from the trees again, charged the fence, and leaped easily over it. Betsy didn't comment.

They had perhaps ten minutes before probable discovery. More if they were lucky, less if unlucky. And a few more minutes for the pursuit to develop actively. In that time they had to accomplish the second phase of their escape.

John led the way to a forest cache. He scraped away leaves and dirt to reveal a package. He hauled it out, shook it off, and opened it. Inside were clothes of modern Standard type, cosmetic paste and spray, and an ID key. He was no longer shy or awkward, now that the escape was in progress. He had worked hard to assemble these supplies and knew exactly what to do with them. So did Betsy. They had discussed this thoroughly by code correspondence.

"Hurry," he said. "I'll spray you, and you spray me. It has to be all over, because they'll probably check." He began to undress.

"I'm not stripping in front of any boy!" she said.

John exploded with exasperation. "Do you want to escape, or don't you?"

She looked at him coldly. "If you were smart, you'd have come prepared. I have already sprayed myself where it doesn't show." She pushed back one sleeve to show him where her white skin turned brown. "All I need is the paste for my face and hands."

She was right, but it didn't make her any easier to get along with. She had taken a terrible chance, wearing Standard brown while traveling with her folks! "All right. You go behind a tree and change, Miss Modest. I'll change here."

She sorted quickly through the clothes and lifted the feminine set. Standards didn't actually differentiate the style for the sexes—it was part of their absolute-nondiscrimination culture—but physical differences required modifications. Thus his brown tunic was larger and wider, hers shaped for feminine contours. She took the paste and left.

John, though he wouldn't admit it to her, was relieved. He hadn't wanted to strip before a girl but had feared she would ridicule him if he hesitated— exactly as he had ridiculed her. Or tried to.

He threw off his clothes and turned the spray on himself. The brown mist bathed him in cloud, then dissipated as the coloration settled on his body. In a moment he was Standard, skin-deep. The moderns used this tan-brown makeup to conceal trifling variations in skin shade; some were naturally darker than the established ideal, and some lighter, so some were considered aesthetic deviants. It was very important, it seemĕd, not to be a deviant, even marginally. It was good dye; it would last for several days without retouching and would not harm the skin. He had stolen the can and other supplies by rifling an open-air dispensary. He wasn't proud of that particular foray, but he had had to have the goods.

Later he had found the functioning identity key. Apparently some Standard had lost it and had forgotten to have the account closed out, or perhaps there had been a bureaucratic oversight. John had used the ID to obtain several random items and had watched for any consequence, but nothing had happened. Maybe no check was made unless a large bill was run up. He had been very sparing, anyway, saving it for an emergency. Now he strung its cord around his neck, for it might be his most valuable possession in the next few hours. Finally he put on his tunic and slippers.

Betsy emerged. She was completely Standard now. Even her hair was darker and shorter—she must have cut it just now, somehow. And she had done something to make her face seem fuller. He had to give her credit: She had obviously practiced this changeover thoroughly.

"Aren't you done yet?" she demanded.

"You have the paste," he pointed out. He would not have had time to use it yet, but it was a perfectly decent excuse. The paste had to be used on hands and face, because it was more substantial and better able to withstand wear and weathering.

She handed him the jar. "We'll have to hide our old clothes," she said.

"No. Watch." He bundled them together and tied them tight. "Canute!"

Canute jumped up, tail wagging.

"Hide this." He proffered the package.

The dog sniffed the bundle, snorting a bit to discover Betsy's scent, then took it in his mouth, tossed it about to get a better grip, and ran off into the forest. Betsy was silent.

John smeared the paste over his face and neck and chafed it into his hands. It was impossible to overstain, so he just had to be certain that he didn't miss a spot.

"Don't forget your hair," Betsy said.

"I haven't." But he *had*. He rubbed the paste over his scalp and worked it around, then recombed his hair.

They had no Standard chronometer, and their watches had had to go in the bundle. The antique timepieces would have been an instant giveaway. But John didn't need to look at a watch to know that their safe margin had been exhausted. From this moment they both were Standards—or else.

He kicked leaves over the hole where the cache had been. "Let's go. We can't hurry, and we can't go in a straight line, because——"

"Stop telling me things I already know," she snapped. "Do you think I'm stupid?"

They meandered away from the region of the fence. At any moment the Standards' spy-beam—or whatever it was—might pick them up. They were gambling on the chance that it was keyed into the unpainted whiteness of their skins or the cut of their clothing, not to anything internal. Maybe a blip showed on a screen, locating them, and a human operator checked when anything looked odd. This escape would tell the story; if they got away, John's guesses were correct.

It would look odd when no blip appeared anywhere on the Newton township screen, but the operator wouldn't know what had happened. Not right away. And when he scanned in earnest, all he would find would be painted whites inside, and maybe a couple of misplaced Standard tourists outside. He hoped.

There was a noise in the woods—a kind of pounding and crashing, as of a large animal coming toward them. Betsy gripped his arm nervously, for they were weaponless. But it was only Canute, returning from his clothes-hiding mission. With that realization the noise seemed to diminish; it had been the mystery that made it loud!

As the dog bounded into sight, John had a horrible thought. It would be difficult for a scanner to pick out John's true-white skin from among false-white skins in the zoo. *But suppose it was oriented to the dog?* There was only one such animal in Newton, so this would be easy to identify, and Canute was never far from his master.

Now John heard the roar of a motor, coming from the same direction Canute had been.

"They're following the dog!" Betsy whispered, catching on in the same instant. "That darned animal!"

5

Gomdog

"Strangers!" John shouted at Canute. Had he subconsciously anticipated this problem? "Play strangers!"

"Your dumb, stupid, traitorous dog!" Betsy said, beginning to cry in frustration. " 'Well, he's coming!' you said, and now look at what——"

"Shut up!" he whispered fiercely, unable to explain his plan.

She glared at him but obeyed. Canute stopped about fifty feet away and sat down. He seemed to be paying no further attention.

A jeep crashed through the forest. It caught up to them quickly and stopped. A whitewashed Standard got out while a second stayed in the vehicle with the motor running.

"Bluff," John whispered to Betsy, lips hardly moving. Then, to the man: "Who are you, Stan?"

This was one of the useful minor things he had learned in the past year. All people were Standards, but it had not always been so. "Standard" was less a description than a designation of courtesy, and "Stan" was the politest title for a stranger.

The man seemed surprised. Perhaps he had thought he had run down his quarry and now might be mistaken.

"Dear," Betsy said, taking John's arm. "They're not Standards!" She pulled him back as though frightened—a very simple role to assume in the circumstances. "Look at the color. White!"

"Don't insult him," John whispered with enough force to carry. "He may have been ill."

"Maybe it's contagious!" she whispered back, retreating farther.

The Standard paused in perplexity. John could guess the man's thoughts: Here he had followed the dog to the zoo specimens and found instead two Standards . . . maybe. Should he explain his unusual coloration or check their ID's! A mistake could be awkward, either way.

"Do you own that . . . animal?" the Standard finally asked.

"Own?" John asked in return, putting confusion into his voice. That wasn't difficult, either. He saw the trap, for there was no ownership of anything in this society, and there were no pets.

"Over there," the man said, pointing to Canute. The dog maintained his distance.

"That vicious creature?" Betsy put in with more enthusiasm than strictly necessary. "It came chasing after us with all those ugly spots and jagged teeth. . . ."

"What *is* it?" John asked apprehensively.

The man looked at Canute again. "Bring him here," he said to his companion. The other man turned off the motor, got out of the vehicle, and approached the dog. Canute growled and retreated. The man made a gesture, and the dog yelped. John saw with a pang that the man had some kind of weapon. Not a gun—but something. Canute yelped again and ran from the man. John kept his face frozen, knowing that this was a crucial test. If he gave himself away. . . .

Another gesture, and the dog stopped short. it was as though he were being herded by an invisible goad. Tail between legs, Canute slunk toward John and Betsy. He looked appealingly at John.

"Don't bring that strange animal here!" John cried, accenting "strange." Canute could pretend not to know his master, when playing this game, but he could hardly understand what was going on now. He wanted protection and comfort, and these were the last things John could provide, lest he betray their whole escape.

Canute struggled with conflicting impulses while all four people waited tensely. Then the man with the goad—it was a little sphere with buttons, held in one hand—nudged the dog closer to John. Canute looked at John and growled.

Bless him! He was playing it out, refusing to admit that he knew his master. Canute had come through, and now there was no immediate evidence that these were the escapees.

"It's attacking!" Betsy cried. "Horrible thing!"

Canute growled at her, too, this time with more authority. She retreated.

"All right, Eogan," the first man said. "It doesn't know them."

The other put away his implement, and Canute ran away.

"Sorry, Stans," the man said. "This is restricted property. Citizens are advised to remain well clear."

"We were only taking a walk," John said, offended. "We lost our way. Then that—animal came. And you, with your—no offense—remarkable coloration, in a vehicle that must be three centuries old. It is—alarming."

"Alarming!" Betsy echoed tremulously.

"A misunderstanding, Stans. We are on a special mission requiring this costume, offensive as it may be to your sensitivities. You should depart the area promptly."

"We shall certainly do so," John said. "If you can direct us. . . ."

Betsy took his arm again. "We had no idea. . . ."

"Proceed southwest, and you will intersect the perimeter shortly," the man said tersely. "I would summon a taxi for you, but no such vehicles are permitted here.''

John proffered the arm Betsy had already taken, and they walked hastily away. Then John halted. "Southwest?"

Betsy caught on at the same time. "What nonsense is this?" she demanded. "Do they *want* us lost?"

"Your pardon, Stans," the man called after them. "I gave you an obsolete designation. My error."

Error, hah! John thought. It had been a parting trap, to learn whether they understood twentieth-century directions.

The man pointed out the correct route. Fortunately they had not been going southwest, owing to the distractions of the moment. That had been mighty close!

"After that gomdog," the first Standard said as the two men climbed back into their jeep. "I hate this inefficient, atmosphere-polluting contraption! If only we were allowed to use contemporary equipment here. . . ." The jeep started up and roared away.

Gomdog? Canute? Was that what they called the tree-climbing dog? The men had carefully avoided identifying it until they were sure they were addressing Standards. Gomdog.

"Funny zoo," Betsy murmured.

Funny, indeed! If the perimeter guard was this curt with spectators, it couldn't be much of a show.

He had at times been uncertain of the zoo notion, and this magnified his doubt.

"They may keep watching us," he said, and she was silent.

John was roughly familiar with the region, of course, and knew that the Standard's advice had been correct: Southwest was the nearest perimeter of the larger zoo environs. So he guided Betsy southwest, following the second, gestured, instructions. He didn't know what system the Standards normally used to orient maps, but it wasn't American. North and south applied only to the zoo itself. . . .

They walked for fifteen minutes as rapidly as the terrain permitted, then came to a break in the forest. Now they had to deviate; John silently guided her northwest, hurrying. If the spy-beam were on them now. . . .

They came to one of the glossy octagonal buildings with stuck-on cubes. This one was empty. John had scouted it carefully and discovered that it was occupied only in winter, but it remained functional the year round. They walked up as though they owned it, and John put his ID to the entrance panel. The panel became foggy—real fog, not just fog color—and he climbed through, hefting himself up to the floating floor level inside. Then he held the ID in place and reached down to assist Betsy. The door panel became solid as soon as he removed the ID key.

"Oops, almost forgot," John said. He ID'd

outside again, put his fingers to his mouth, and made a piercing whistle. Almost immediately he heard Canute's answering bark. In moments the dog came racing into sight, greyhound lines with spots. His tongue was out, he was panting heavily, and his fur was streaked, but he seemed all right. John held the door permeable while Canute leaped through.

"Oh, no!" Betsy cried with dismay. "They'll follow that animal to us again!"

John hugged the big dog to him while Canute licked his face between tail wags. "They'd have caught us already if he hadn't led them a false chase," John said. "Good dog! You did great! I'm proud of you. Punch for a taxi, Betsy. By the time they catch up, we'll be gone. Yeah, you're my dog, Canute!"

"Second fiddle to a dog!" Betsy muttered. "If he was female, I'd know what to call him!" She poked experimentally at the house's communications console. There was a hum. "Taxi, this address, immediately."

"Your ID, please," a voice said.

"Here," John said quickly, passing over his key. Betsy touched it to the appropriate panel.

Standard communications were efficient. A sphere dropped from the sky within seconds and touched the house, tangent at the door panel. John used the ID again and passed with Canute directly into the vehicle. Betsy hastened to join them.

"It worked!" she exclaimed, gratified. "I really called a taxi!"

"You just get us to that third zoo you saw. I'll see about the dog."

"See what? He's already here, unfortunately."

"They called him a gomdog. Maybe I can find out something."

"Oh." She located the taxi's communicator, then paused. "What do I tell it? I saw that spot on the map, but I don't know how to locate it. I can't tell this buggy to fly north. . . ."

"Um." John had supposed they would pilot the craft manually, but one glance at the control section showed him that it was nothing like anything he was acquainted with. They couldn't afford time to practice—not while the Standard pursuit was near. "Try this. 3777767256."

"What?"

"It's a coordinate. Ala gave it to me."

"Who?"

Suddenly he realized that he had never had a chance to tell her about the black girl or to inquire whether Betsy had met Humé. "Yesterday—look, it's complicated, and we're in a hurry—I met a girl. . . ."

Betsy stared at him. "You, too? I wasn't going to tell you right away, but——"

"You met a black man!"

"Black? *Yellow!* His name was Yao Pei, and he lived—*lives* in Northern China, eighth century A.D."

"Chinese! Mine was African!"

"And there's at least one other purebred there," Betsy continued. "A girl named Meilan."

"This thing is more complicated than we thought," John said soberly. "We've got to compare notes—but, Betsy, there just isn't time now! They may be on our tail already. We have to find those others quickly, or we may never have another chance."

"You're one hundred percent right, for once. Give me that number, slowly—or better, speak it into the communicator here. Maybe the taxi will take us there."

John agreed. "Taxi, take us to coordinate 3777767256, and step on the gas."

A voice replied, different from the one at the house. They both jumped, and Canute perked up his ears. "Step on the gas is not a programmed destination. Please clarify."

"Do all their radios talk back?" Betsy inquired.

"What I mean is, hurry!" John said. "To that location. The number." Would the taxi do it?

The globe sailed upward, sending John stumbling and Betsy grabbing at handholds. The first hold she found was Canute's tail, and both parties were outraged. Then the taxi shot over the landscape.

Boy, girl, and dog picked themselves up. "When it hurries, it *hurries*!" John exclaimed. "We must be doing two hundred miles an hour!"

"Ridiculous," Betsy said. Then she reconsidered. "At least!"

John peered out and down. For the first time he saw the Newton township in its entirety and the lay of the land about it. Now he could compare his zoo to the reality that lay beyond. There was no discernible difference. It was *all* field and forest. Newton was no oasis; it was typical, so far as the terrain went. He tried to conceal his disappointment; he had been almost sure that there would be a substantial and striking change once the Newton environs had been left completely behind.

"You were seeing about the dog?" Betsy reminded him snidely.

"Right away," he said, nettled again. She was certainly running true to form. Here they had important business to accomplish and astonishing experiences to compare, but she couldn't stop needling him about Canute! The white-colored Standards of Newton had never been like this, he reflected. He had sometimes railed, privately, at their lassitude; he wanted to see some spirit, some human animation. Now he was faced with plenty of both—in Betsy—and didn't much like it.

He faced the communicator. "Information," he said, as though he were using a telephone. He suspected that Betsy would have had greater confidence with this sort of project, but it was his baby. He *did* want to know the truth about his dog, if the truth was to be had.

"Well, go ahead," she told him. "You asked for information."

He had expected some acknowledgment. But of course this was the twenty-fourth century. There would be no inefficient lags. "Gomdog," he said. "What is a gomdog?"

"Synopsis," Betsy said quickly. "Otherwise you may get hours of——"

"Synopsis. For the layman."

"Gomdog," a pleasant voice said. "Colloquial designation for sapient psuedo-mammalian species of GO 'M' III. Vestigial technology, competent adaptation of form, pacifistic temperament." The voice stopped. John sat stunned for a moment.

"Did you hear that?" Betsy demanded, shocked.

"A complete alien!" John said. "A creature that changes its shape——"

"No. The other. "It said 'sapient.' *Sapient!*"

"So?"

"Dummy! That means intelligent! Human level, or better."

Intelligent! John looked at Canute, appalled. Had his faithful canine companion been fully aware all along? How could they hope to make their escape with this creature watching?

"He's a spy!" Betsy said fiercely. "I knew it!"

"He can't be," John said, defending Canute, though he felt sickly uncertain. "He's always been loyal."

"Loyal to *whom*? A zoo specimen? We'll never get away with him along. Get rid of him."

"Kill Canute? I'd shoot myself first," he said, believing it.

"I didn't tell you to *kill* him. I said get rid of him. Dump him out, turn him loose—just so he can't spy on us anymore."

John looked at Canute again. The dog—the gomdog—just sat there and wagged his tail questioningly.

"Maybe it's just another trap," John said. "They used that word where we could hear it so we'd think he's a spy and get rid of him, and then we'd be on our own, and they could catch us."

"Do you believe that?" she demanded derisively.

John avoided a direct answer. "If he's intelligent," he said slowly, "he knows everything already. We can't afford to let him go—and it would be illegal to kill him, even if we had the guts for it. If he's not intelligent, we don't *have* to get rid of him. So. . . ."

"Casuistry. If he's sapient, we can't afford to keep him with us. If he isn't, we don't need him."

John knew he was grasping at a straw but could not help himself. "We don't *know* he's a gomdog. . . ."

"He's either that or something else just as bad. Certainly not a real dog. Ask the machine—you'll see."

"What is a dog?" he asked information. "Synopsis."

"Dog: colloquial designation for extinct mammalian canine species of Sol III. Former domesticant of man. Quadrupedal——"

"Extinct," Betsy interrupted, and the information narration cut off as she spoke. "So this one *has* to be something else. And you can bet it doesn't look like a dog or act like it in its native state. *Now* are you satisfied?"

"No. I can't believe Canute would betray me. Us. I don't care what he is biologically, he's my dog."

"He's an alien spy, but he's your dog. Great!"

"A gomdog made into a real dog. Information: Would he betray his master?"

"Data insufficient," the voice said.

"If he had been taken as a puppy or whatever it was and taught to be a dog, and he associated with one person like that for a year and a half—a real dog would never do anything to hurt that person. Would a gomdog?"

"Data insufficient."

John contained his frustration, knowing Betsy would smirk if she saw him express it. "What do you need to know?"

"Protein content of gomdog's diet. Diversity ratio of training. Preconditioning. Planetary environment. Pedigree."

Betsy became interested. "Gomdogs must be more special than we thought."

John was nervous now. He did not look at Canute. "He ate a lot of table scraps. He was supposed to stick to dog food, but he likes everything, and I'm softhearted."

"Soft*headed*," Betsy muttered.

"I guess it was a high-protein diet. Why is that important?"

"Sapience of the species is directly affected by early diet."

"As with human beings, too," Betsy said. "And probably all living things. That means he's smarter than he's supposed to be. Because you fed him wrong."

"I *like* him smart!" John snapped. "Diversity ratio of training—I didn't train him much at first. We were just pals. Then later I showed him how to do all kinds of tricks, like jumping fences, hiding things, playing 'stranger'—I guess it was pretty diverse. And he learned awfully quickly. I even used to read him stories, just for the fun of it, and discuss my homework."

"That means you gave him a good education," Betsy said. "You really set out to dedog him, you know."

He ignored her. "I don't know about preconditioning. I guess he was told to act like a dog. He was a week or two old when I got him—pure white, no spots at all. There can't have been much else, at that age—I mean, how much can a week-old *anything* learn? But he always did *look* like a dog. I guess his pedigree is normal—a gomdog is a gomdog, isn't it? And the planetary environment is earthlike."

"So would this gomdog betray his master?" Betsy asked.

"Qualified answer," the communicator said. "Assuming unmodified purebred stock, ad hoc conditioning with proper reinforcement, diverse but informal training—gomdog would be capable of willfully betraying his associates but would be unlikely to do so without extreme provocation. Probability eighty-four percent."

"Probability of *not* betraying is eighty-four percent?" John asked tensely.

"Correct."

Betsy crowded John away from the communicator. "How smart would it be?"

"Eighty percent of human norm, fifteen percent margin of error."

"So Canute has an I.Q. between sixty-eight and ninety-two!" she exclaimed. "And it may be even more if some of those assumptions are wrong." She turned to John. "He may have been given super-potent food, you know. Why would they leave a thing like that to chance? He may be as smart as we are!"

"I doubt it," John said cautiously. "He's smart, but not that smart."

"You *hope*! He could be smart enough to conceal his smartness from you. How would you know?"

That stumped him. "Well, if he is, he's still loyal. What's wrong with being that smart?"

"As if we hadn't just gone through all that! He might make a very bad enemy."

"So *that's* what you're driving at! Did you ever stop to consider that he might also make a very good friend?"

"*Your* friend, not mine."

John stared at her. "You're jealous of a *dog*!"

"Don't be ridiculous!" But her flush gave her away.

"Why didn't you bring *your* pet?" he asked.

"Carry a birdcage along on a jailbreak?" she demanded witheringly.

"I thought parakeets could be trained to stay close without being caged."

"Mine *was*—inside. Outside it would have flown away."

"Oh." He felt awkward. "I'm sorry." Then: "Was it a real bird?"

"I don't think so. Not an earth bird, anyway. Let's not talk about it."

"Well look—you can make friends with Canute. It isn't as though——"

"Forget it," she said sharply.

For a while they rode in silence, watching the monotonously green landscape passing below. John estimated that they had come over a thousand miles already, for the taxi had accelerated to super-jet-plane velocity and maintained it. He had yet to see a city or even a town the size of Newton. There were no roads and few fields. Only occasional shapes—octagons?—that might have been factory buildings except for their complete lack of smoke or access. Apartment houses, maybe—he had picked up mentions of these. Giant complexes of octagonal residences with shared sanitary and culinary facilities. Why the Standards should prefer to live in such constricted warrens, when all this unused countryside was available. . . .

"I'm sorry," Betsy said. "Try asking information at what age a gomdog matures."

John shrugged and inquired.

"Eighteen years," information replied.

"Eighteen years!" John was astonished. "That's about the same as *us*!"

"Not surprising, if it is as intelligent as we are," Betsy said. "You can't mature in a year and know everything someone else has learned in ten or fifteen."

"But then Canute is still a puppy—his mind would be like that of an eighteen-month-old human baby. Even if he's going to be as smart as us, that's a long way off."

She nodded. "So call him a dog."

John was immensely relieved. "I'm forgetting what I started out to do!" he exclaimed. "We have to change Canute so they can't spot him anymore."

"If the scan is visual."

"It is for *us*. When we changed clothing and color, they didn't know us."

"We're *human*. An animal might have a bug implanted. Something to home in on."

"So we're human. We could still be bugged the same way. Why should they bug the dog when it's *us* they want in the zoo?"

She spread her hands in overelaborate bafflement. "Ask information."

But at that point they felt a shift in course. They were coming down—to the coordinate of the third zoo? They exchanged glances, but neither cared to suggest what they might encounter there.

6

The Walled City of Wei

John spotted it first. "That's no American town! It's a walled city!"

Betsy looked. "That's Wei!" she exclaimed. "Pei's city! What a coincidence!"

"One chance in five," John pointed out. "Really, one chance in two, since we're obviously not heading for your place or mine or Ala's. So it was really an even bet that we'd strike pay dirt—if the coordinates meant anything." He looked again. "And I guess they did."

"Oh, shut up. Your reasoning is ludicrous." But she remained pleased. John decided that Yao Pei and his residence must have made a strong impression on her, and he felt a tinge of jealousy.

"Why don't you call him by his first name?" he inquired.

"Pei *is* his first name. His given name, I mean. The surname comes first, in China."

John contemplated the massive brick ramparts, the tall corner towers, and the handsome tiered roofs of the enclosed buildings. This city· was formidable and beautiful. No wonder it had impressed her.

For a moment he was afraid the taxi would land outside the wall, because they were coming in very low. The barrier was a good twenty-five feet tall, surrounded by a moat, and almost as thick as it was high, to judge from the depth of the main gate. The top was crenellated, providing excellent cover for riflemen—no, *archers*, he corrected himself—and the great gates seemed impervious. But they passed over and dropped at last into a central park. No need to storm the bastion!

But why hadn't the Standards installed some kind of electronic warning system, to prevent twenty-fourth-century taxis from straying onto these secret premises? Had John been running the show. . . .

John and Betsy looked at each other again, and he realized that he was running a show of his own—and had planned no better for it. "We can't just walk in," Betsy whispered, as though her voice could betray them. "I don't know my way around. I never really saw the city like this. I was unconscious or something when I—"

"I know."

"And we're stained brown, not yellow."

That was another awkward detail. "How do we

tell who is real? This is much larger than Newton!
There must be a thousand people here!''

"I'll recognize Pei.''

"Sure. And all the men of this Oriental metropolis will just parade by the taxi so you can pick him out!''

"You don't have to be sarcastic!''

She was a fine one to talk! "Sorry,'' he said, not sorry.

"They're coming,'' she said, peering out. "The Chinese.''

Catalyzed by that pressure, John came to a decision. "Canute can find the real ones. I'll run interference. You take the taxi up out of danger until we're ready.''

"I don't know how to operate it!'' she wailed.

John knew what she meant but had no time for sympathy. "Don't get hysterical. You don't have to operate it. Just tell it any coordinates, then tell it these ones when it's time to come back.''

"I can't remember the number!''

"Here.'' He grabbed for a pencil to scribble the number—and came up against the empty cloth of his tunic. For an instant he was baffled; then: "Information will remember it! Just ask!''

"How do I know when it's time?''

The man shapes were coming quite near, and she *was* becoming hysterical. He realized she was making excuses to avoid going by herself.

"Guess!'' he shouted. "Give Canute something to smell—something Pei touched. *Hurry!*''

Hands shaking, she obeyed. She brought out a tiny object from a little purse she had salvaged from her other clothing. "Cowrie shell," she said, holding it stiffly down for Canute. "They use them for money. . . ."

"Canute! Find that person!"

The dog sniffed, woofed, and wagged his tail.

"Let's go!" John cried. He held the key before him and leaped through the door, Canute beside him. Too late. The yellow-colored Standards were already there: two men in ground-length, belled robes.

"Who are you?" one demanded. "Don't you know no spheres are allowed in the enclave? Suppose *they* saw it?"

"Go find!" John whispered to Canute, slapping him on the flank. The dog bounded off.

"Hey!" one of the challengers cried. "What's that?"

Then the taxi lifted.

As the two men stared in dismay, John slipped away.

"Hey!" the man cried again. "You, Stan!"

John ran. That was the idea: As long as they were chasing *him*, Canute could search the city without undue interference. Of course, John had to keep from getting caught himself, and then he would have to bring the two Chinese purebreds to the park, unobserved, and hope Betsy timed it properly—if she didn't lose her nerve entirely.

.

"Stop!" the man called. "You're not painted! If *they* see you. . . ."

John swerved between bushes, jogged down a flowery footpath, half-crossed and half-hurdled a small decorative bridge, and ran into the city proper. The pursuers fell behind.

Suspicious, John slowed and looked back—and saw them walking nonchalantly.

Of course! They did not dare raise a loud hue and cry, because that would call attention to the "Standard" running loose in the city. If the two true Chinese took note, the whole zoo project would be in peril, particularly after the mix-up that had already introduced the Chinese boy to white American Betsy. On the other hand, the pursuers would be unlikely to give up, and more would undoubtedly close in as the word quietly spread. They might use that same knockout weapon that had put him away when he was with Ala. (Was that only yesterday?) And they were familiar with the city, whereas he was not. So he'd better lose himself quickly.

John sprinted down the street, turned a corner, and almost crashed into a roadside fruit stand. Oranges, bananas, pineapples, assorted melons, and others he didn't recognize—he was hungry! But he didn't have any money, or even cowrie shells.

"Papaws—thirty cash," the vendor began, then did a double take. "Standard! Get out of here, before——"

"I'm an inspector," John said without premeditation.

Confused, the vendor let him pass. John turned another corner, dodged down a narrow alley, turned again, and came up against the city wall. This place—Wei, Betsy had called it—looked large only because it was strange. It was actually only a few hundred yards across.

A sentry paced along the top of the wall. John ducked back out of sight, stifling his loud-seeming panting, but found that he had nowhere to go. The street had no close offshoots, and the houses here were like blank screens: impassive and forbidding. No porches, no windows. Even their front gates were shielded by smaller walls.

But he heard people coming behind him. By now there were a number, and they had a pretty good idea where he was. John ran back toward the wall, hunching low so as to avoid discovery by the soldiers there, and found what he had prayed for: a space where the slanting wall surface parted from the vertical house surface. He scrambled in.

By this time Canute should have located the real Chinese, Yao Pei and his female counterpart. Maybe the dog was already on his way back, to pick up John's own trail. All he had to do was hide and wait and let Canute sniff him out. But *where*? He couldn't get into any of these formidable residences, and even if he could, it would only raise another shocked cry from the owner.

One slipper turned against a piece of rubble in the crevice. John jumped and caught himself by spreading his arms against the walls on both sides. If he got a foot jammed here. . . .

He intersected another street. His hands were filthy, and his tunic was badly smudged, but neatness was nothing compared to his giveaway color and clothing. Should he walk down this block, hoping that he would not be spotted? No—that would be begging for trouble he couldn't afford.

As he hesitated, a man emerged from a house a short distance along the street. He wore the usual sandals and robe and appeared to be middle-aged. For a moment John was tempted to charge up and hijack him, taking his clothing for camouflage, but he realized almost at once that he couldn't do it. He had neither training nor temperament to attack a man—particularly an innocent bystander.

He heard a noise behind him, back on the other street. Prodded by that, he ran toward the man.

"Friend!" John cried, improvising as the other turned to face him. "I got put down in the wrong zoo—er, place! I need some paint, some proper clothing. Before *they* see me!"

The man looked disgusted. "*Another* mistake! This is ridiculous." Then he had a second thought. "Which enclave uses Standards as such?"

Oops! "I mean I was supposed to be processed for the Caucasian one. But somehow . . ."

"I understand. Come inside, quickly. I'll give you a period costume and some paste for your face and hands. Then you can be a traveling bard just leaving the city. *They* may never even see you. And if they do—well, we do get quite a turnover in the lesser personnel here. Your face doesn't have to be familiar."

John followed him in, gratified that his problem had been solved so readily. "I—I really don't know anything about *this* enclave. What is it? Where— *when* is it?" He did know a bit from what Betsy had said—just enough so he would know if the man tried to lead him on.

"Middle Kingdom. Twenty-eighth year of Hsüan T'ung. We're supposed to be about a day's hard ride from Changan, the T'ang capital. Of course there isn't any, but *they* don't know that."

Don't bet on it, buster! "Middle Kingdom? I'm trained in twentieth-century American geography." He hoped the man wouldn't catch on how literally he meant that. "Can you transpose to—to the Gregorian calendar?"

"Gregorian? I'm not sure. When does it start?"

"Birth of Jesus Christ, approximately. My enclave is dated about nineteen sixty—about two thousand years after that."

"Ah. Christianity! That hasn't penetrated here significantly yet. Let's see—your sage lived during the Han dynasty—somewhere around the reign of Wang Mang, I believe. But Christ was in one of the barbarian Western states. The Roman? Or was that Muhammad?"

"No. Muhammad was about six hundred years later, in Arabia." John paused, just now remembering an obscure bit of lore he had picked up from his historical studies. *The Moslems started their dating with Muhammad!* From the time he left Mecca, rather than his actual birth. John had been required to memorize that date: A.D. 622. Now he was thankful for that chore. That meant that the date of Ala's enclave was six hundred years later than he had supposed. Between A.D. 1500 and 1600.

"So this must be about seven hundred fifty by the Christian scale," the man said. "Seven hundred forty, perhaps."

"And your 'Middle Kingdom' means China? Not ancient Egypt?"

"Naturally. Many cultures had 'middle kingdoms,' but the T'ang dynasty is the most civilized place and time in all earth's history," the man said with a certain pride. "Pre-Standard, of course."

"Of course." So this was what China was like twelve hundred years ago. T'ang dynasty—John remembered it only faintly from his classroom lessons. Famous for painting, or something. "What do you do here?"

"I'm a civil-service examiner. I administer the hsiu ts'ai and send the results in to the emperor every year, and every three years the chu jen. Those are rough tests, too. Most applicants are eliminated by the hsiu, and only one in fifteen passes the chu. Of course it isn't real, except for *him*."

"You actually tested the purebreds?"

"The true Mongolian, yes. Yao Pei, that is. The girl isn't eligible. I supervise all the tests. The records have to be genuine, you see, just in case.

Keeps me busy, but I rather like it. It's a meaningful task, in its quirky way, and that's important. A man needs meaning, you know?"

"Yes." Did this mean there was no meaning in conventional Standard existence? Very interesting.

As they talked, John was being fitted with full Chinese apparel. "What's your job to be, in your own enclave?" the man inquired.

"Well, I haven't started yet, of course," John said, scrambling mentally for a suitable answer. "But I'm supposed to be a—an auto mechanic. Transferred in for the bus station." That should hold him, since there were no cars or buses—or, indeed, any machines at all—in ancient China. No internal combustion engines, anyway, and probably very few in the Standards' home territory, either. Not when they had such advanced equipment as the flying taxi-spheres. So chances were that this civil-service examiner wouldn't know enough to ask penetrating questions.

He was right. The man concealed his ignorance by fetching a jar of yellow paste. John hoped it would go on over the brown paste he had used not so long ago. "The real one—did *he* pass the tests?"

"Yes, strangely enough. Yao Pei is astonishingly knowledgeable, considering that he's had what we assume is a typical period schooling. I sealed him into his cell myself, so I know he spent the full three days as prescribed, without food. To him it was real, you see. I gave him obscure topics from the literature of Confucius, but he composed fully satisfactory poems—almost perfect styling. Amazing."

"You sealed him into a cell? For a *literature* test?" John didn't have to pretend astonishment. Meanwhile he studied himself in the bronze mirror. He looked Chinese.

"That's the way it's done. In the real Middle Kingdom the aspirants sometimes died from the strain. But it was the only route to status and the official posts. So we duplicate it faithfully. I myself feel that is has its merits, for you can be sure that no weak man passes. But of course it also leads to intellectual arrogance and narrowness of thought. I am certain that this was the root of the downfall of T'ang and all subsequent Middle Kingdoms. In fact"—the man brought himself up short. "I'm waxing philosophical again! Must curb that."

John had been rather interested in that philosophy, as it seemed to apply to a certain degree to his own schooling. He had not had to take his exams in locked cells without food, but he *had* had to parrot a fair amount of unoriginal lecture material. "Curb it? Why?"

The man laughed, a little nervously. "Why, indeed!" Then he changed the subject. "When Pei passed the hsiu, I rejoiced, but when he later mastered the chu jen, I began to fear. And I only hope he does not pass the last one, the chin shih."

Suddenly John's attention flagged. Was that a scratching at the front gate? Canute must have arrived!

"Thank you very much," he told the man. "I'd better go before my ignorance of this culture calls attention to me. If you will direct me to the gate. . . ." Yes—it *was* Canute.

"Yes, that's best. The perimeter guard will pick you up once you leave the enclave, and you can explain what happened. It was bad enough before, when that Caucasian girl landed here! None of us knew what to do. The program was almost hopelessly fouled up, so she visited the Pei for a couple of hours until—" He broke off and shook his head. "But so far today Pei hasn't said anything, so maybe it's all right, though he's dangerously clever. These blunders certainly have to stop!"

"They certainly do!" John agreed heartily. He tried to think of a way to get more information on the purpose of the enclaves from this helpful man, but there wasn't time. "I really appreciate your help. I'll find my own way out."

"Oh, I'll start you on your way. I can point out your first turn, so you can"—he paused as Canute's whine grew louder—"something's out there!"

"You must be mistaken," John said quickly. Then, so as to cover any other sounds the dog might make, he had to keep talking. "I really should go by myself. Suppose *they* happened to be in the area and saw a stranger talking to the civil-service examiner? *They* could get suspicious."

"I'm sure *they're* not near here," the man protested. "And it will be much more efficient for me to show you——"

"I'm so glad you understand," John said, reaching the door at last. "Make a left turn at the next intersection and——"

"A right turn—at the second intersection, not the first. Then straight on to the main gate. But——"

"Thank you once more. Good-bye." John stepped quickly out, closing the door in the man's face.

"Good-bye?" The muffled voice came. "I don't——"

"Sorry; that's a Caucasian enclave expression." Canute was there, tail wagging. "Hide!" John whispered fiercely at him.

The man forced open the door. "I must show you. . . ."

John stood in his way, blocking the running dog from view. "Oh, was I in your way? I'm sorry." He moved to get in the man's way again, as though accidentally.

Somewhat flushed even through the yellow coloration, the examiner finally made his way out the door, but Canute was gone.

"I must say, you have a natural aptitude for barbarism," the man observed, almost losing his Oriental presence. "Your facial contours, too, resemble the Caucasian. You are an excellent selection for that enclave."

John was aware of the man's sarcasm, but he could hardly blame him. He listened with un-Caucasian patience to the examiner's concluding remarks and finally went his way alone. What a tangle!

The dog reappeared at John's whistle and led him back into the city, disappearing whenever they encountered other people. No one recognized John as the Standard intruder, perhaps because of those un-Standard facial contours of his. At last they stopped at an attractive house with yellow walls and a red roof.

"Here? Both of them?"

Canute wagged his tail.

"How do we get in? Without alerting the natives, I mean." The dog would not understand his words but should pick up the gist from the tone.

Canute trotted around to a hidden section of the sidewall. He dug his claws into the sunbaked brick and began to climb.

"Hey! I can't follow you there!"

The gomdog went on climbing. The wall was about twelve feet high on the outside. Canute disappeared under the extended red eaves while John waited in frustration below. He had thought the dog understood—and now this!

Then Canute's nose reappeared. There was something between his teeth. A tug and haul and a length of rope dropped down.

"Good boy!" John caught the end, jerked it to be sure it was anchored, and hauled himself up the wall. He threw a leg over the top and scraped his torso under the roof. The brick did not actually support the roof, he saw, nor was it the whole wall. There was a rammed-earth filler inside and then a wooden framework. Beams rising from this met the ceiling. The perch up here was not comfortable, but it would do.

The rope was securely knotted around one of the wooden uprights. John was sure Canute could not have done that. Who, then?

Canute crawled along a beam for a few feet, to where the rising roof left a larger space. It was dark and distressingly hot here. Then he shifted over to a dark square well—a ventilation shaft?—and climbed down into it. Cautiously, John followed. He could tell by the sounds Canute made that the hole was not deep, and he was able to drop down with only a slight thump. This landing must be on an upper story. One side of this space was wood, but another was cloth. A large blanket or rug hung down, and specks of light showed through it like stars. Canute sniffed the air for a moment, then pushed past the edge of the curtain.

John's eyes had just adjusted to the darkness, and now the return to light was painful. But he squinted and followed the dog from one room to another. He was aware of painted wooden walls and ornate tapestries and elegant sculptures and bamboo furniture and knew that this was the house of a wealthy man. An official, probably. Then there was a courtyard, neatly laid out, with unfamiliar flowers around the edges. He wondered fleetingly whether they could be poppies—opium poppies.

"Who are you?"

John jumped, though the tone was quiet. Before him was a Chinese youth about his own age but more slender. John parried with his own question: "Are you Yao Pei?"

"I am." The other looked coldly at him, waiting for an explanation.

"I'm—I'm John Smith. I——"

"Show me your hand."

Surprised, John held out one hand. Pei took it and rubbed something on the palm. The yellow faded, showing the brown of Standard disguise. Pei looked down at it, then at John, not deigning to speak.

"Rub some more," John said quickly.

In another moment the brown gave way to the pink-white, and no further rubbing would change it. "So the dog did not betray me," Pei murmured.

"That was your secret entrance he sniffed out?" Suddenly it made sense. If Pei were as smart as reputed, he would have his own exit—and Canute, following the smell, would naturally have found it. A hidden rope!

"Do not speak," Pei said. He left the room, gesturing John to remain.

So Pei had made the connection to Betsy! He had to know that there was only one Caucasian boy available and what John's purpose had to be, and he would certainly be aware that he was watched much of the time.

Pei returned with a girl. She was lovely—a delicate Oriental aristocrat, poised and serene. She wore a garment of bright silk, embroidered with a portrait of a silver unicorn. Iridescent feathers decorated her copious black hair. A jeweled sash fit closely around her slender waist. Her feet were tiny.

"Meilan, go with this man," Pei said.

She only nodded.

John looked at Pei, wanting to ask his plan, if any. Pei gestured toward Canute.

"Stay," John murmured to the dog. "Lead him."

Canute looked unhappy, but he obeyed.

Meilan took John's arm and guided him firmly through the house. They saw no one, though John was sure others were near. Somehow Pei had arranged it so that there was no suspicion. Betsy must really have briefed him! They went down narrow steps and out the front gate. So the house was not on two levels; its main floor was raised.

Outside, John thought it was his turn to guide her, but she would not follow his lead. She insisted silently that they go north, away from the park. When they were out of sight of the yellow building and alone on the street, Meilan reached up to remove her pretty feathers. Then she undid her waist clasp and opened her silk dress. It came off suspiciously easily—and underneath was a rough gray shawl. From somewhere she produced a pair of clumsy sandals and put these on her miniature feet in lieu of her fancy slippers. She combed out her hair and tied it in a crude knot.

She had converted into a peasant girl in less than a minute! John marveled that this outfit should have been concealed under the fetching, tight-waisted party dress. She must have been fighting for breath!

Now she let him lead. In fact, she bowed her head as though she had just been beaten and insisted on staying behind him, nullifying his attempts at courtesy. He felt as if he were leading a slave. She was so servile and disheveled!

They walked at a moderate pace toward the park, ignoring the occasional people they passed. Probably most of the city was concerned with the Standard intruder spotted earlier, he thought, and could not be bothered with unrecognized bit players. The city would be bothered tomorrow, though, when it discovered its prizes gone!

But they would have to wait at the park, for Yao Pei had not arrived with Canute, and Betsy had not brought the taxi back. John became increasingly nervous as he realized how critical the element of timing was and how dependent they were on sheer luck. If Betsy arrived before Pei, or if the Standards figured it out and intercepted them. . . .

John glanced at the peasant Meilan. Betsy might have briefed Pei, but how well had Pei briefed Meilan? Or had she picked up something from the boy she must have met, if this foul-up had been consistent? That would be—well, if white John had met black Ala, and white Betsy had met yellow Pei, yellow Meilan would have had to meet the last, Ala's intended—black Humé. Humé of Kanem. What had passed between them?

"A Standard taxi will come—there," he murmured, flicking his finger toward the interior of the park. "You understand?"

Her expression was enigmatic, but before she

answered, a farmer turned a corner with his donkey. The animal hauled a rickety cart loaded with dead fish and live scraggly ducks. The smell was potent, for the fish were not fresh, and the birds had obviously been caged without sanitary measures for some time.

"You look like a person of quality!" the peasant man exclaimed, bearing toward John. "Fine fresh fish caught just this week, excellent geese!"

"No, thanks," John muttered, trying to avoid him. The man's face and arms were smeared with dirty grease, as though he had been wallowing in his merchandise.

"Behold this spectacular bird!" the farmer cried, jerking open a cage and hauling forth a bedraggled duck by the feet. "I trapped him just this morning on my own fields. Yours for only one tiao. A fantastic bargain!"

"Thank you, no," John repeated, wishing the man would go away. Betsy's taxi could arrive at any time, and there would be no chance for secrecy if they had company. They could wait for Pei only if unobserved.

"You drive a hard bargain, master!" the farmer bellowed. Even his breath stank of fish. "But I'll let you have him for only two thousand cash."

Meilan made a stifled sound, and John realized he was being bilked—assuming he intended to buy at all. He didn't know how much a tiao was, or two thousand cash, but either was probably far more than the bird was worth. "I don't want any," he said with some force. "Go away."

The farmer stared at him from a round, smudged countenance. "Do you want me to lose face?" he demanded in return, not budging. "Do you despise my fair merchandise? I shall have to complain to the prefect!"

Meilan covered part of her face with one hand. Oh-oh. Translated, that meant the Standards would learn something was up. John remembered that "face" was very important to the Chinese. Everything had to be done in such a way as to preserve the appearance of self-respect. He would have to play the game, even though he knew it *was* merely a game.

"I did not mean to disparage your merchandise," John said carefully. "I am merely out for a walk and do not need a duck. I did not wish to waste your valuable time." The valuable time of a fake peasant!

The farmer considered. "All right. Let's be friends. Have supper with me." He lifted a dirty bag from the cart and went to sit on the grass at the edge of the park. "Come—join me. I have excellent stewed rice, bamboo shoots, fermented bean curd, pig gizzard, and plenty of cold tea. All grown from the finest natural fertilizer—men's own."

John's appetite left him. "I, uh. . . ."

"You don't want to be friends? The prefect. . . ."

Brother! The farmer's filth-encrusted hands were already dumping out the comestibles—all mixed together. Not only was it an unappetizing meal, it meant he was not going to get rid of this nuisance at all soon.

Meilan's shoulders were shaking, and her face was averted. John couldn't blame her for being upset. To have this happen *now*! Seeing no alternative, John joined the farmer on the ground. He succeeded in refusing the bamboo shoots but not the bean curd. This was an almost cakelike mass—and, surprisingly, it did not taste bad.

Meilan continued to avert her face, but she nibbled daintily at a bamboo shoot. John watched the interior of the park nervously, hoping the taxi would not come. Yet.

"Ah," the farmer sighed happily. "This reminds me of the feast of Hsu Chen-Chun Ching-Chih after he bested the dragon, the spiritual alligator."

"Who?" John asked without thinking.

"Hsu Chen-Chun Ching-Chih, whose ordinary name was Sun. You do not know of him?"

Should he say yes or no? John decided on the truth. "No. I mean, yes, I do not know of him."

"Wonderful! I shall tell you the entire story!"

Meilan made a strangled sound. John cast about desperately for some pretext to prevent the threatened narrative, but the farmer had already started.

"Sun was a native of Honan, born in the time of the Three Kingdoms, some five hundred years ago. Ah, there was a marvelous, romantic time!"

"Yes, I'm sure," John said impatiently. How could he get rid of this loquacious peasant? The whole escape was in peril.

"What a man! Sun, whose full name was——"

"Get on with the story!" John said, muscles twitching.

"With pleasure, since you ask. During the great drought he had only to touch a fragment of tile, and it became gold and brought wealth to the suffering people. By his magic talismans he cured sickness. During the dynastic troubles of San Kuo——"

"What about the dragon?"

"Why hurry the tale? It is not yet even dusk."

"I'm eager to know the outcome," John said despairingly. Where were Yao Pei and Canute?

"Very well. Seldom have I had so attentive an audience. In the Lu Shan Mountains south of Chiu-Ching was a dragon, the spiritual alligator. He transformed himself into a young man named Shen Lang and married Chia-yu, the daughter of the chief judge of T'an Chou. In the winter he lived with her, but in the spring and summer he returned to the country to roam in the rivers and lakes as a dragon. One day Sun met Lang and recognized him as a dragon and knew at once that—" John looked up as the farmer paused. Soldiers were coming! Three of them—and he could tell by their attitude that they were looking for someone. And here he was with Meilan, snared by a storytelling farmer! It was too late to hide.

"Have you seen *them*?" the lead soldier demanded.

"Why, yes," the farmer cried, though the question had been directed at John.

The troopers gathered round, bows at hand,

arrows bristling from quivers, swords naked. John's heart sank. The weapons might be primitive, but they were plenty adequate for the occasion!

"Here?" a soldier demanded. "How long ago?"

"At the yellow house this very morning," the farmer said proudly. "I saw *her* arrive, and I tried to sell her a live goose, but"—he paused, seeming to think of something—"here, let me show you my wares. Look at this exquisite bird! Only one tiao, because I so respect men of the sword. And fish too—just smell that aroma!"

The soldiers had already smelled. Noses wrinkled, they retreated.

Meilan was choking. John permitted himself a smile. This was a silver lining he had not anticipated. No one would bother them while this peasant had merchandise to peddle.

But what had held up Yao Pei and Canute? This was getting more serious as time passed. If Betsy came now. . . .

"That he was the cause of all the floods that had been devastating Kiangsi Province recently," the farmer said, picking up exactly where he had left off. "Sun decided to get rid of Lang so that the land would prosper again. But the dragon was aware of this. He changed himself into a yellow ox and fled. Sun transformed into a black ox and pursued him. The yellow ox became tired and jumped down a well to hide, but the black ox saw him and jumped in, too. Seeing this, the yellow ox jumped out again and escaped to T'an Chou where he resumed human form and lived with his lovely wife."

"Why didn't Sun follow him?" John demanded, irritated at both the interminable tale and its inconsistency of detail. "If *I* chased a yellow ox like that and had him trapped in a well, I'd keep my eye on him better than that!"

Meilan seemed to be on the verge of tears as the farmer remarked to John, "Perhaps you have better eyes than Sun. You would not be fooled by any disguise."

"Oh, go on with the story!"

"Sun, perceiving that Lang had gone, climbed out of the well, returned to town, and assumed human form. He located Lang's house and stood outside, addressing him in a severe tone of voice. 'Dragon, how dare you use a borrowed form, pretending to be a man?' But there was only the sound of Lang's children scurrying about the house in fright."

"His children!" John exclaimed. "How could he have children if he was really a dragon?"

The farmer gave him a knowledgeable look. "Dragons are quite virile creatures, in any form."

"That isn't—I mean, genetically—"

At that point the taxi appeared in the sky, heading for a landing in the park. Betsy was returning, and Yao Pei and Canute were still missing! To make it worse, the farmer saw it, too—and the three soldiers were running back toward the park. It would be impossible to wait.

"Canute!" John cried despairingly. "Canute! Come here!"

Dead fish flew up as the dog appeared, charging through the farmer's cart. Canute had been waiting for the call all the time!

"Into that craft!" John shouted at Meilan. "You, too, Canute." They all ran headlong for it as it landed.

For a sick moment John was afraid he'd left his ID in his Standard clothes, but he hadn't. He had hung on to it automatically, and the examiner who had helped him had not questioned it. After all, all Standards had ID's.

He held the key before him and Meilan and Canute struck the door almost together. The panel fogged to let them through, and they sprawled in a pile on the taxi floor. "Take it up!" John cried.

Acceleration sent them sprawling again. John banged his face against the wall and was oblivious to his surroundings temporarily. About the time he decided that his nose was bent but not broken, something else registered. There was one person too many in the taxi.

He sat up and looked about more alertly, and then gaped. "What are *you* doing here?"

The talkative peasant-farmer smiled. "So you would know a yellow ox?"

"Yao Pei!"

Then they all laughed while Canute licked the smell of fish from his fur. He had been buried under the livestock in the cart, where absolutely no one would care to look. . . .

7

Chase

"Where to?" Betsy inquired.

"The enclave 0544071364," John said. "That should be where we'll find Humé, and Ala should be with him."

"Well, feed it in. You know I can't remember those numbers just like that." She turned to Meilan. "You must be——"

"Yes," Meilan said. "Is there a basin of water?"

"There's a Standard sanitary cubicle. I just figured out how to use it myself. Let me show you." The two girls stepped into the cubicle and sealed it off, leaving John alone with Pei.

John took care of the destination and waited for the taxi to adjust course and steady down. "It may be a while," he said. "Now, you sly chameleon, *finish that story*!"

Pei smiled, unperturbed. "Sun cried again: 'Come out, or I shall surely send soldiers in to kill you!' And he summoned spiritual soldiers to surround the house. Then Lang transformed back into the spiritual alligator and came out defiantly, thinking himself invulnerable to attack. But the immortal soldiers harassed him, and he flew away and was never seen again. Then Sun made Lang's two sons come out. He took a mouthful of water and spurted it on them, and both became young dragons who also fled. Finally Sun told Chia-yu to vacate the premises. He cast a spell on the house and it sank beneath the earth, leaving a lake where it had been. After that Hsu Chen-Chun Ching-Chih, known as Sun, assembled the members of his family, all forty-two of them, and they all ascended to heaven. Even the dogs and the chickens went along. Sun was then a hundred and thirteen years old. After that a temple was erected in honor of him."

"But what about the feast?" John demanded. "You said he feasted! That's what reminded you of the story, you claimed. But he didn't feast—he went to heaven!"

"So did we," Pei said blandly.

The girls came out. Meilan was much improved, now looking like neither aristocrat nor peasant girl, but very pretty.

"I'm starving!" Betsy said. "Can we put down somewhere for a meal?"

Yao Pei reached into his rags. Slowly he brought out a long-dead fish. "Build a fire," he said.

Canute snorted. Betsy looked annoyed, then reversed herself and laughed. "But I *am* hungry. If only—" She stopped. "What's that?"

John caught a motion from the edge of his vision. "Oh-oh. Our luck's run out."

Another sphere was following them, and it was gaining.

"Well, you couldn't expect to raid another enclave in a modern antigrav taxi without attracting attention," Betsy said, but her voice shook a little.

"The advantage lies with us," Pei said. "We should be able to outmaneuver them."

"I don't see that," John said. "This is an ordinary taxi, as far as we know. That may be a police-sphere, with more power. And they'll be skilled at handling it. And others may intercept us. We may have to drop to the ground and take our chances in a hostile terrain. They have the advantage, any way you figure it."

"You misunderstand. We can outmaneuver them because we have less to lose than they do. We can take risks they cannot—and they will not press us very hard."

"Maybe common sense is different in the Middle Kingdom. *Why* won't they press us hard? *Why* can we take risks they can't?"

"Consider the investment they have in us. Without us the enclaves are meaningless. Almost twenty years of time, and all those properties and personnel, wasted, if we should die."

"Die!" Betsy exclaimed, shocked.

"All that effort and expense wasted," Pei repeated. "So they will be exceedingly careful."

"But if—why should we risk our *lives*?" Betsy demanded, shaken again.

Pei turned on her the same calm gaze he had used on John in the park. "Our lives in captivity are not valuable, are they?"

The other three paused. John saw that none of them had thought of it precisely that way. Escape had been more of a game, without anything really serious—such as life itself—at stake.

"So what we are risking is very little," Pei continued. "We want to be free. Living in captivity may not be worse than death, but it is not a great deal *better*. We would be well advised to put our entire resources into the effort for what we desire and believe in, and they know that. They know that if they press us too hard, we may tumble and perish. Then they will have lost everything. But if we escape, they can always hope to find us again later."

"That does make macabre sense," John said. "So you think we can get away—if we have the nerve to do it."

Pei nodded.

The other craft was closing the gap. There could be only a few minutes before it caught up.

"*Do* we have the nerve?" Betsy asked in a small voice.

"We'd better decide in a hurry, or they'll nab us

while we're debating it," John pointed out. "Why don't we vote?"

"Vote?" That was Meilan, looking perplexed.

"That means each person says what he chooses, and the majority decides it."

"Strange system," Pei remarked, "but I choose to escape."

"So do I," John said. "What about you girls?"

Betsy hesitated only momentarily. "Yes."

They looked at Meilan. "I would prefer to recover the others," she said.

"The others?" John repeated.

"The people in the other enclave that we were going to fetch. Humé."

So she *had* met Humé! "I didn't mean to desert them!" John said. "Certainly we should pick them up. That's where we're headed now, but we'll have to lose that police cruiser first." Pei and Betsy nodded.

"Then, yes."

"Hang on!" John cried. "I'm putting this buggy on manual, and I don't exactly know what I'm doing!"

The manual control was a ball set in a magnetic clasp. When activated, it hovered within the little cage, touching nowhere. It was transparent with a gray opaque spot on top. Inside it he could see another shell, translucent red. Inside *that* was a third shell, translucent yellow, and so on. Somehow he was able to see the color of each level merely by concentrating on it. That would have been a very

neat trick by the standards of twentieth-century
earth. Here it was just a fixture.

When he switched over, the taxi stopped. Just
like that. It hovered in place, and the pursuing ship
gained at an alarming rate. Hastily, John put one
finger on the surface of the ball and juggled it. The
taxi rocked violently in the air. John grabbed for a
handrail. The others laughed; they were already
hanging on.

"There would be three primary axes of rotation," Pei said, hauling himself near. "Test each
one cautiously."

"Gotcha. I can push the spot forward or backward or to either side, or I can spin the ball
around." He put his finger on it and nudged the
gray spot ever so slightly forward. The taxi descended slowly.

John pulled the spot back toward him, with a
little more confidence. This time the taxi rose, with
fair acceleration. He saw that the inner spheres
remained in place, and now a dark-red spot showed
on top of the translucent red sphere, uncovered by
the gray one.

"Vertical control," Pei said. He sounded calm.

"And *hurry*!" Betsy said, not calmly at all.
"Another thirty seconds, and they've got us!"

John let the spot center, then nudged it to the left,
rolling the ball sideways in place. This time the taxi
moved left, speeding up as he turned farther. Now
yellow showed at the top, from the next shell down;
the red had stayed under the moving gray.

"Horizontal," Pei said.

John held the spot over and pulled it toward him. As he did so, the red one came into view, and the taxi rose at an angle.

"Vectors!" John cried. "The spots show each force acting on the vehicle! We're moving left and up, so the resultant is a slant. Terrific!"

"Now rotate," Pei suggested.

"Ten seconds," Betsy cried, watching the pursuit. "Nine, eight, seven. . . ."

John let the ball go, then spun it clockwise. The taxi shot backward, sending them all tumbling again, but this time John hung on. He saw the pursuing sphere pass them thirty feet below, surprised by this late maneuver.

"All right, crew! I've got the system now! Latch on to the furniture, 'cause we're going to dive!" He turned the ball forward until it was upside down.

They were weightless as the taxi dropped. Then he spun the ball counterclockwise, and the sphere raced forward at the lower level.

"They're on manual, too," Betsy cried, still watching. "They're looping around to come at us again."

"With a second craft," Pei said.

John held the ball spun half around to maintain speed, noting that a green spot showed on its side. Green was forward velocity! He pulled back to show the red dot, lifting the vehicle, then turned right to expose the yellow. Now he was going forward and up and left, all at a good clip.

"They are enclosing us," Pei said.

John saw. Two more spheres had arrived, and probably more were on the way. Each craft was now about a hundred yards distant from the taxi.

"I can sling this ball about a bit," John said. "It would be rough on us, but I might shake one or two of the others. But a swarm——"

"That does affect the probabilities," Pei admitted.

"Want me to drop down and hide in the bush?"

"They'd run us down before we got far," Betsy said. "Look!"

A fifth globe was hovering directly above them, matching ascent and velocity.

"And there," Meilan said.

The sixth globe was below.

"We aren't going anywhere," John said. "That's englobement."

As they watched, bands of light began to develop: four glowing streaks, emerging from each craft and touching the adjacent ones. The beams linked them all in a double pyramid, with the taxi centered where the bases met. Eight glowing triangles fenced in the fugitives.

"What are they doing?" Betsy asked, worried but intrigued.

"Building a birdcage," Pei said. "I suspect the walls are more substantial than they appear."

"A cage of light!" John mused. He was too fascinated to be frightened. "Well, let's give it a try!"

He accelerated the taxi toward the open center of one of the huge triangles of force. Light sparkled as they touched the geometric plane. The taxi shuddered and slowed, bathed in the glow. Its power remained on, but a greater power brought it to a stop.

"The beams are only where it shows—in a direct line between ships," Betsy said. "At the corners, or whatever."

John reversed and brought the taxi back to the center of the cage. "The net must be everywhere, though. We're trapped, all right. Not even any chance for heroics."

"If I may suggest," Meilan said. "There is a game played by the boys of my province——"

"A game!" Betsy cried disdainfully. "We need a cannon!"

But John remembered Meilan's cleverness in converting from one costume to another. She was a sharp girl, and her notion could be worthwhile. "What game?"

"They would mount and ride toward each other, guiding their horses aside at the very last instant. The first to swerve was——"

"Chicken!" John cried. "I've heard of that with cars!"

"I do not know of cars, but a chicken is a bird," Pei said. "And we are now a caged bird, but——"

"Not that kind," John said excitedly. "What they did was pack two cars—horses, in your case—

full of kids and charge 'em down the highway at each other head-on. Sometimes neither one would swerve, and then it made headlines; but usually. . . ."

Pei looked at the spheres surrounding them. "A test of courage. I begin to understand, foolish as it seems to me."

"It's a game we can play, all right!" John said. "You explained why before—and this time it *isn't* foolish. Close your eyes, folks!"

He oriented the taxi and zoomed it forward, directly toward one of the englobing craft.

"Hey! You'll crash!" Betsy screamed.

"That's the idea," John said, but he was beginning to sweat. He continued to move at increasing speed, centering directly on the selected target. "Coming at you, Standards!"

The other globe swelled alarmingly as they rushed toward it. Then Betsy cried out incoherently and ran at John, but Pei intercepted her and held her back. Meilan still did not move or speak. They closed to fifty feet, traveling at what John judged to be almost a hundred miles per hour. Betsy began to scream, piercingly, as they smashed into the— She finished her scream on a note of surprise. They had passed through without colliding.

Pei smiled grimly. "They were, as you say, chicken."

The other sphere had dodged out of the way in that last fraction of a second. The network of force had been disrupted at that point, and the taxi had broken out of the cage. The bird would not be trapped like that again!

"Now will you let me go?" Betsy asked Pei.

"If I must," he said, smiling.

"Know any more games like that?" John asked Meilan. She only smiled.

The six spheres had been foiled, but they had not given up. They were now following about a mile behind, keeping pace but not gaining. John was not pushing the taxi to its limit, so he was sure the pursuit was deliberately holding back.

"They do not wish to play again," Pei said. "But we cannot proceed to that other enclave so long as they are watching us."

"We have to lose them somehow," Betsy agreed.

"I have heard that ships can lose each other in fog," Pei said. "Especially in a storm."

John followed his gaze. "That's just a cloud formation. Hardly a storm."

"Storm!" Betsy said, turning to this new topic with enthusiasm. "Let me turn on the weather report."

In a moment she had the taxi's communications screen on. She experimented with its controls, searching for weather.

John felt something at his hand. It was Canute's nose. "Yeah, we've been ignoring you," he said, patting the long head. "Dog or gomdog, you're still my pal. I'm sure glad you weren't lost in China!"

"Here we are!" Betsy cried happily. "A continuous weather report. And look—they have a large storm scheduled! If we can locate it. . . ."

"Worth a try," John agreed, though he had strong private doubts. A civilization with technology this advanced should have no trouble tracing a taxi in a storm.

"And I can read the coordinates!" Betsy said, elated. "Except they have only five digits apiece. Must be a different grid."

"Ask information," John said. "We don't have to figure out coordinates when we have that."

"Take us into the nearest rainstorm," Betsy told the communicator.

The taxi shifted back to automatic and changed course. The six following globes matched the change but did not close in again.

Pei's gaze was fixed on the communicator. "That spirit in the machine," he murmured to John. "It can understand what we say?"

"Yes. I think it's like a computer, with a big bank of information. It can answer questions and——"

"It was constructed and given life by the Standards?"

"Of course."

"Should it not serve its masters, then?"

"You don't understand. It's a *machine*. It——" Then John caught Pei's meaning. *The Standards could be listening in on everything.*

"Betsy," John called. "Turn it off." He gestured toward the communicator.

"Turn it off? We *need* that." Then she, too, caught on. "Ouch! We're prime fools, all of us!"

She fiddled with the knobs. "I hope that does it. Can't be certain, so——"

"So keep it low and simple," John said. "I think we need a change in plans."

"We could land in the storm and all jump ship," Betsy whispered. "And send it on to somewhere else. They might follow it."

"We need the vehicle," John pointed out. "We don't have a chance of finding Songhai or whatever without it."

"We can't keep it," Betsy said. "By this time they must have traced that ID, and they'll know every time you use it, maybe. We *have* to take our chances on the ground."

"Maybe that's what *they* think. We might drop ourselves right into a trap on the ground. At least they can't catch us here."

"Perhaps we could do both," Pei said. "We could drop somebody to check the enclave while the others went on. Then we could rendezvous at a set time and place and see which course looked better."

"Yes!" John agreed. "In fact, we could set down at a dozen places, and they might not know where we got off, or if we did at all. We can fool them yet!"

"But who checks the enclave?" Betsy asked. "*I'd* much rather stay with the taxi."

There was a pause. Evidently they all felt the same way.

"I have Canute," John said finally. "He would

be a big help on a ground mission, so I suppose I should do it."

Nobody argued with him.

"Well, let's firm up the plan," Betsy said, visibly relieved. "We drop you, loop around, come back— but if we do it too soon, you won't have a chance to fetch them, and if we come too late. . . ."

"Same problem we had before," John said. "I'm not anxious to time it that finely again, though I guess it wasn't as close as I thought, since Pei was there all the time."

"There are two coordinates left," Meilan said. "Humé told me about the numbers yesterday. We should check them both."

"I know which one is Ala's," John said, "but she won't be there; she'll be with Humé. So there's no point in——"

"But we can't assume the *other* coordinate is Humé's," Pei said. "It might be Meilan's or——"

"No," Meilan said. "It is Humé's."

"That's an interesting confusion," Pei said. "We do know where we're going, but perhaps the Standards don't. They may know we have coordinates. If we set down first at the wrong one. . . ."

"It'll act as a diversion! Canute and I did that before, and it seemed to work."

"Perhaps you should go to Ala's enclave, then," Pei said. "I will go to Humé's."

So Pei was volunteering, too, when it counted. John was both disappointed and relieved. He had wanted to find Ala himself, but he didn't want to undertake another tense search so soon after the last. "Good enough. Let's break out the paste and spray so we can convert to Standard in a pinch——"

"I don't think they'll be fooled that way again," Betsy said. "And you already have two layers of color on you. It might start peeling or something."

"I suppose so. All right; let's make this look good. Drop me about five miles north of the enclave, so I seem to be sneaking in. Come back a couple of hours later five miles south of it; that's when we don't want Standards watching."

"You'll need more than two hours, then," Betsy said. "You can't go ten miles on foot *and* search the enclave in that time."

"Make it four hours, then. And—what time of day is it? At night we could make a quick light. . . ."

"We won't know the time until we get there," Betsy said. "It might be halfway round the planet on the dark side."

"And Humé's enclave might be another half-planet from *that*! This is getting complicated!"

"Perhaps we must revise our plan again," Pei said. "We must be certain of our two remaining purebreds."

John sighed. "Yes. Drop me at Humé's. Then if you can't check the other enclave in time, come back. Our timing must be right."

"We will set down again five—is it miles?—south," Pei said. "Or at dusk, whichever comes later."

"I can estimate the miles," Betsy said. "It won't be exact either time, but if he makes a light—are there flashlights here?"

They checked. There were none.

Now the taxi was entering the storm region. Wind and rain buffeted it, and the pursuing craft were soon hidden.

"I hope this is half as difficult for them as it is for us!" John said. "I'll look for a light in the enclave. If nothing else, I'll make a fire. Somehow."

"Suppose it doesn't work?" Betsy asked. "I mean, if you can't find them, or you can't make a light, or the Standards catch on. . . ."

"If there's any trouble, don't even try to pick me up. No sense in having us *all* caught. I can try to trek overland to another rendezvous. Uh—we'd better decide on one."

"Why not an empty enclave?" Meilan said. "They would not look for us there."

The others paused. "You're right!" John said. "They'd be sure we'd stay well away from the zoos! We could hide there indefinitely."

"But which one?" Betsy asked.

"Let me recommend my own," Pei said. "It is well protected, I know where the supplies are stored, and we all know where it is."

They exchanged glances. "I guess it's agreed," John said. "Okay, let's put down somewhere along here in this rain, so the Standards think we're getting out, then bounce over partway and do it

again, and finally pass near Humé's enclave and
drop me and Canute. By that time the Standards
should be thoroughly confused. They can't make a
thorough search of every place we stop—I hope."

They gave the taxi the coordinates again but put
it on manual twice to make the decoy landings. The
six following spheres seemed lost in the storm but
reappeared in place as the taxi emerged from it.

"That's good, I think," John said. "Means
they're locked on the taxi, nothing else." He
checked himself over nervously. "I'd better take
some spray and paste along, even if it doesn't take
well after so many layers. So I can mix in with the
natives. The painted ones."

"Better leave your ID," Betsy said. "We can't
operate the taxi very long without it—can't even get
out of it!—and you won't need it in the enclave."

John turned it over a little sadly. He was no
Standard, but he felt a bit naked without it.
"Somebody better practice with the manual controls," he said. "It will confuse the Standards about
our target area, and it's good stuff to know."

"Yes. Let me try," Betsy said. She switched to
manual, and they clung to the rails while the taxi
did its dance. John felt simultaneously seasick and
hungry, to his surprise.

After that they took turns, swooping the vehicle
around with greater enthusiasm, while the six
pursuers matched them maneuver for maneuver
with dismaying accuracy. But they came nearer to
the assigned coordinate, for one of the taxi's

registers was evidently a distance-from-target indi-
cator, and the figure was diminishing. Miles,
yards—they could not know what units were being
shown, but when the number was down to zero,
they would be there.

"Funny—they don't seem to use eights or
nines," Betsy remarked. But the rest were too busy
watching the pursuit to verify that.

"There it is!" Meilan cried suddenly, pointing.

Sure enough, there was a group of white squares
that could be buildings.

"But we aren't there yet!" Betsy said. "According to the distance numbers, there's still a way
to go."

"Maybe the speedometer is out of whack," John
said, his voice sharpened by tension. "That's an
African enclave—see, some are round grass huts.
So just drop me north of this one, on manual. And
make sure you can find this place again!"

Pei took control and guided the taxi down. Trees
loomed. "Don't land," John cried. "Just hover a
few feet up, as though you're just changing direction; I'll jump. Get ready with that ID, Betsy."

Pei's handling seemed clumsy; then John realized
that the wobbles were deliberate, so the Standards
would think the near approach to the ground was
accidental. "Time!" Pei announced, bringing the
taxi to a halt in midair. Betsy poked the ID at the
door, dissolving it.

"Come on, Canute!" John cried.

Canute came charging. Meilan happened to be

standing between the dog and the door. She stumbled as he banged against her leg. She grabbed automatically at him for support, falling toward the door.

"Look out!" John cried, but the available space was small, and he was already dropping himself. Canute's momentum carried both dog and girl into the door panel and through. All three fell in a rough tangle and struck the ground hard. John spit the dog's soft black ear out of his mouth and lurched to his feet while Meilan rolled lithely aside.

The six craft were too close. There was no chance to put Meilan aboard again. Betsy and Pei must have realized this, for the taxi shot away.

Meilan was along on this mission, perforce. "Hide!" John cried.

8

The Empty
Enclave

John dived under the nearest bush and saw
Meilan doing the same. Canute had already disap-
peared. They waited while the six craft passed.
None landed; none hovered.

"It worked!" John said at last. "They think
we're all still in the taxi!"

"Um," Meilan murmured from inside the brush.

He got up and dusted off his bruises, then went to
help her. "Sorry you got caught in this. Are you
hurt?"

"No," she said, looking after the departed
spheres.

"Well, you'll have to come with me, I guess.
Here—you can use the brown paste if you like."

"I prefer to remain as I am."

He shrugged. "Okay. How are you at walking?

We have five miles to go if Pei figured it right. The faster, the better.''

"We of the Middle Kingdom are philosophic about hardships."

He wasn't certain whether she was joking, so he started walking. Canute led the way at a stiff pace, even for John, and he was in excellent physical condition. Meilan fell behind, but not far behind, and did not complain.

It must have been less than five miles, for in half an hour they were at the barrier fence of the enclave. It was not wire. It was a palisade—a fence of strong wooden stakes, each sharpened into a spearlike point at the top. Every so often there was a taller stake with a human skull mounted on the apex.

"If I were an African, I think I would be terrified," John said appreciatively. "As it is, I'm none too confident."

"It is no worse than what the northern nomads do," Meilan said. Again, John was not certain how she meant that.

He cast about for a suitable pole but found none. "I could probably hurdle this," he explained. "It's no more than five feet high in places, because of the lay of the ground. And Canute can get over, too. But you. . . ."

"If you lift me," she said matter-of-factly. "A lady is not supposed to know such arts, but I was never a lady—not after I knew about the Standards."

"But we don't dare touch that fence. It may be—"

"Yes. I will not touch it."

With misgiving he bent and laced his fingers together, letting her put one tiny foot in this stirrup and hoist herself up. She did not weigh much.

"Now you heave as I jump," she said.

He heaved; she jumped. He watched amazed as she sailed up and over the palisade, flipped about in the air, and by the sound of it landed on her feet cleanly. This was no delicate Chinese flower!

John chose his spot, made a practice rush, then ran back and up to hurdle the stakes. "Come, Canute!" he called as he landed, and the dog followed.

Inside, they advanced cautiously. The land here was grassy and open. The soil was reddish and spotted with light-green bushes, patches of forest, and rolling fields. The air was hot; John was sweating, and he could see that Meilan was uncomfortable. Canute ran ahead, enjoying it.

But where were the people? There should be Africans laboring in these fields, and elephants. . . .

John stopped to investigate a cultivated field. "Millet, I think," he said. Meilan didn't comment.

In due course they came to a town. Now they had to duck behind any cover available, alert against discovery. Their yellow skins would be an instant giveaway. It was nervous, tedious work.

Near the fringes were round huts with clay walls and roofs formed from large leaves. The three sneaked between these, but still neither saw nor heard anyone else. Canute sniffed the air and found it fascinating but showed no alarm.

"Where *are* they?" John whispered.

Farther in, the houses became square, with flat roofs. These were larger and in better condition. In the center the buildings became quite large and considerably more ornate. Some looked like storehouses, some like forts, and some like palaces, but all were made of clay.

There was no doubt of it now. The town was deserted. There were no people and no animals.

"I think we're in the wrong enclave," John said. "This must be Ala's—and they closed it down the moment she went to join Humé."

"She is important to you," Meilan said.

Surprised, he denied it. "I simply wanted to find her and Humé and get them out of here."

Meilan half smiled and dropped her eyes.

"Well, we have a couple of hours to kill," he said. "Nothing we can do here. Wonder where they keep the food?"

"I will look," Meilan said. She stepped into a towering mosque. Wooden spokes projected from it in lines at several levels, showing where the flooring supports were for the upper stories. Overall, the building was like a giant cactus, topped by a tall minaret. It seemed ungainly at first but was also impressive and a little frightening, this artifact of a foreign religion.

John started to follow her, then decided to hasten the search by choosing another building. He doubted that the fancy structure would have much inside that was edible, but if there were a granary. . . .

Something caught his eye as he walked down the unpaved street. A motion in the sky. A travel-sphere! "Hide! Hide, Canute!" he cried as he dived for the nearest doorway. If the Standards were coming back, he and Meilan were in trouble!

He couldn't go to warn her, for the sphere was in a position to see most of the street. He peeked out and saw it hovering above the town. That was the giveaway, for it would never have come like that if the enclave were still in use—unless all pretenses were being dropped. This certainly wasn't the taxi. Had the Standards caught on? Would they descend and make a ground search? Had the others been caught, so that now only he and Meilan were free?

Canute looked up at him in perplexity, aware of his alarm but not comprehending its reason. John patted the furry head with empty reassurance. He had to do something! Frantically he ran into the main section of the building, looking for some sheltered exit so that he could make his way to Meilan. If she stepped out into that street now. . . .

He was in a palace. The walls outside might be of drab clay, but the bricks had been dried hard and well fitted, and there were patterned mats hanging inside. The effect was elegant, and he wished he had time to properly admire the colorful designs. But the thought of that ominously hovering sphere. . . .

He passed from chamber to chamber, each seeming more luxurious than the last but none leading outside. Then he burst into a great sunken courtyard, almost tumbling down the steps leading to it. Canute began a sniff-circuit.

John peered up cautiously to see whether the sphere was still there. All he saw was the plaited mat of the slanted overhanging roofs and the mural-like decorations around the court. The sphere, if it remained, was hidden by the building. He could not afford to assume that it had gone. In fact, it might be coming down for a landing.

He sidled around under the overhang until he found another entrance to the main structure. "Canute!" he called. "Find the back door. The *back* door."

The dog put his black nose to the floor and snuffled off. John followed. Again he passed through vacant, tapestried chambers. It was amazing how thoroughly the place had been cleaned out, since only yesterday Ala had lived here! This morning, perhaps. But of course they could have started dismantling the sections she wouldn't be seeing, in the last few days, removing the furniture and other accouterments.

Which house, he wondered, had been hers? None of the round or square ones looked comfortable from the outside. Perhaps it was a different story from the inside, as the exotic tapestries here implied. A girl that wore massive gold earrings could hardly live in a hovel. . . .

Abruptly he was outside. Canute had found the

exit. John scuttled for cover again, hoping he had not been seen. He entered another building, ran through its gaunt clay chambers, and finally encountered the clay-covered palisade enclosing the back of the mosque. Was Meilan still inside?

Panting, he ducked through a gateway, slunk along inside the wall, and entered. This interior was dark and cool. He groped ahead. Canute made a little *woof!* of greeting.

"John! Did you find food?"

He jumped, though he had known by the dog's reaction that she was near. "There's a sphere outside! They're looking for us!"

She did not seem unduly alarmed. "If they were sure of our presence, they would be checking the buildings. Perhaps they are merely making sure the village is in good condition while vacant."

This was a sensible analysis, but John was not in a mood to admit it, after his struggle to get to her in time. "We'd better scram!"

She demurred. "I have found a bowl and pestle. We can prepare some of that millet in the field, perhaps."

"We can't prepare anything if they catch us!" he exclaimed.

"We should not go outside while they are watching. If we can find grain inside. . . ."

She was right, of course. If the sphere came down, they could run; if it didn't, they wouldn't *have* to run. And they could not go far while it watched. So it made sense to continue looking for food.

They maneuvered into another building, then a third. There was no grain. "They really cleaned this place out," John said. "The personnel must've taken off the moment school got out. But they didn't destroy anything. Maybe they expect to reactivate it when Ala comes back from her visit, or after her hajj."

"I wonder now," she said, "whether the reason it was so easy to enter here was that they wanted us in the enclave—any enclave."

"*Wanted* us here. . . ." John considered. "Now I *really* want to get out!"

"Yes."

John realized that he rather liked this girl. She wasn't sarcastic the way Betsy was, but that was only part of it. She was different. Smart and decisive in her own way but ten times as subtle. "You didn't fall out of the taxi by accident," he said.

"I thought you would need help."

"I *have* help. Canute."

"An excellent animal."

Meaning that an animal couldn't prevent him from doing something stupid? Or meaning that she liked Canute? He couldn't tell.

They peeked cautiously out and into the sky. The sphere was gone.

"Now's our chance! Let's get out of here and over the fence. We can wait on the other side until it's time for rendezvous."

Meilan agreed silently. Eyes more on the sky than on the ground, they left Ala's village of Mopti, in the great empire of Songhai, 976, or in the 1500s, Christian calendar.

Canute woofed as they neared the fence. They hid and waited but saw nothing. "False alarm," John whispered, though the dog remained nervous. "A snake, maybe."

"Possibly," Meilan murmured noncommittally.

They moved up to the fence, and he boosted her over as before. Then he and Canute hurdled it. A miniature travel-sphere floated into sight just outside the palisade.

"Run!" John cried.

Meilan and Canute took off in opposite directions. John turned to go at right angles to their paths. He found himself headed back into the fence, spun about as the sphere bore down, and put his foot into a hole. He fell headlong, pain shooting through that ankle. He tried to get up but collapsed as the weight fell on his hurt foot. He cursed his own incompetence, but he had never before been exposed to real pain, and his reflexes prevented him from using that foot. By the time he oriented himself the sphere was before him.

A beam of light came out from it, and somehow John lost control over his muscles. It was as though the nerves had been disconnected, making him helpless. He fell a third time. The sphere did not wait for him. It flew after Meilan, weaving in and out between the trees with impressive facility. John tried to call out, to warn her, but his voice would not perform any more than his muscles. He was still breathing, and his heart was still beating, but he

could do nothing on a voluntary basis. She hardly
needed the warning, anyway.

It made no difference. He heard her cry as the
sphere caught up. Then silence. He knew the
outcome. He had not anticipated this nullifying
beam that rendered him unconscious from the neck
down, though he should have. The web of force
that the Standards had placed around the fleeing taxi
had suggested what type of technology they
possessed.

The invisible hold on him loosened gradually.
His arms and legs prickled as though awakening
from circulatory restriction. The pain returned to
his ankle. Evidently sensation as well as control had
been inhibited. He struggled to sit up, and slowly
his body responded. It was like swimming through
molasses (not that he had ever done such a thing!).
He had to exert an infinite force to accomplish an
infinitesimal motion, but the job did get done.

He looked at his ankle. The skin was unbroken,
and he couldn't be sure whether there was swelling,
but he could not put weight on it. Something inside
had been wrenched. Nevertheless he scrambled, on
hands and knees, trying to hide himself before the
sphere returned. He might get away while Canute
led the Standards a merry chase, or he might
distract the sphere long enough to allow Meilan to
recover and hide. Certainly he couldn't give up
now!

It was not to be. The sphere returned, stunning
him again, and this time he lost consciousness
completely.

9

Captives

John woke in lather. He struggled through the
foam, gasping for breath and blinking away the
sting. This was involuntary, as he was neither
suffocating nor hurting; the stuff around him merely
seemed as though it should have some such effect.

In due course the bubbles receded, leaving him in
a warm glowing tank or stall. He saw that his skin
was white again. The foam had washed away the
cosmetics! He had, then, no secrets from his
captors. They knew who he was and what he had
tried to do, and they had stopped him. He did not
even have Canute for company.

Canute! That was his one trump card! The dog
must have escaped and would seek him out. Almost
immediately his flush of enthusiasm diminished,
seeming to ebb with the bubbles. How could a dog

get in here? If Canute approached, the Standards would beam him down, and that would be that.

When the glow had dried him, a section of the wall became bright. He recognized one of the walk-through panels. He had no ID anymore, but these things didn't *have* to be attuned to that, he was sure. He stood up, wincing as his weight hit his foot—but found that the pain was slight. He was hardly lame.

The compartment was octagonal, and now he saw that a panel had opened in one of the walls to show a dry Standard tunic and footwear together with underclothing. John took the outfit and put it on, preferring this to going naked. Strange, he thought. They had washed him white but were dressing him Standard. That didn't seem as though they were going to return him to Newton.

Now he touched the door panel and found it open. He passed through it into a comfortable apartment. Meilan was waiting for him. Canute was with her.

Numbly John surveyed the scene. This was a complete Standard residence, with a sleep converter, communicator, and sundry furniture. The main room was about twelve feet across and octagonal, with a plaque high on one wall bearing the number 32, the number of the apartment. Of the eight short walls he knew that four would abut the walls of similar compartments in one of the Standard beehive complexes he had observed during their long flights in the taxi—unless this happened to be an isolated unit, like the one he had spied near his own enclave.

"I am pleased to see you," Meilan said, maintaining her T'ang reserve. She wore a tunic, too, and looked better in it than she had in her peasant rags. Then: "You're white!"

"I got scrubbed. This is my natural color, you know. That's the bathroom I was in—sanitary cubicle, in Standardese. A square with the corners lopped off by cupboards, so it comes out octagonal, like this room. Have you been here long?"

"About an hour. They brought me in through there." She gestured to the wall a quarter circle to his right.

"That figures. That's the hall door, then. That's open for only an hour, if what I picked up in my pre-escape explorations is accurate. Then the dining room, then the supply closet, or maybe the other way around. I think it just keeps going around like that. You have to time yourself, if you know what I mean."

She looked perplexed. "But why?"

"Because four apartments share each utility. The Standards don't waste anything, not even space or time, though they seem to have a whole planet to exploit. Each family lives in a unit like this, with eight in a row and eight rows. And eight floors. That's what I understand, anyway. Just a big block of five hundred and twelve octagonal chambers, and I don't know how many square spaces between them. Cramped but efficient, I guess. And miles between the buildings—miles of wilderness forest. And no roads. You saw that, too."

"All these huts shoved together?"

"Pretty much. Octagons don't fit together exactly. There's leftover space. That's why they have the little cubicles, though some of them turn into octagons by the time all the fixtures are installed. It would make sense if the Standards had a large population—building things close and tight, I mean—but they don't. They let hundreds of square miles go to waste for every one they use. Which is a paradox, because they're so efficient otherwise."

"I don't like it," she said. "I'd rather live in Songhai."

John laughed, feeling at ease and important as he explained things to her. "Doesn't bother me. Not that part, anyway. All the comforts come right here to your room. Where I get sensitive is about my *mental* freedom. I don't mind living in a small room; I *do* mind being told what to do."

"I have always been told what to do," she murmured. "I did not mind."

"Then why were you so happy to leave?"

"They were not my people."

That much he understood completely.

The bathroom door slid shut. At the same time the door to the right slid open. "Mealtime—for an hour," he said. "If we want it."

"I am not hungry. But I will be before it comes round again."

"Well, I'm famished. We don't know how long

they'll keep us here. Maybe only another hour. Maybe days. In either case I want to fill my stomach. Come on."

They stepped into the dining compartment. "I've never had a chance to do it before, but I think I know how to work this," he said. "You press one of these buttons, like this, then stand back, and. . . ."

A bowl of something that looked like hot porridge rose up through the counter as the surface became fuzzy. There was no eating utensil. He looked at it dubiously. "I don't know how you get a spoon. Maybe something else. . . ."

Meilan reached inside her tunic and brought out a pair of chopsticks. She took the steaming bowl and lifted out a gob. She touched it to her tongue. She smiled.

John was tempted to order another for himself, but he did not know how to use chopsticks, even if he had any. He punched another button at random, hoping for something he could eat without an implement. He was lucky. It looked like a slice of meat loaf, and the taste was not too far off. He used his fingers.

Canute woofed. "Sorry, man's best friend. I forgot you. I guess you don't get too much choice, but it seems to be good food. I'll get you another like mine."

So they ate and, once they found the buttons, drank. "I wonder how Pei and Betsy are doing?"

John said. "They must be pretty hungry by now if they're still in the taxi."

"Pei had a fish," Meilan said, smiling momentarily.

They continued in silence. John found that he had to believe that the others had escaped, for they were the only remaining hope. Surely they would have been brought here, if captured, since he and Meilan and Canute had been put together. So the fact that the others hadn't shown. . . .

But that didn't help the captives directly. If he and Meilan could escape, then they could rejoin the purebreds. John was sure Meilan wanted to escape, too, but he could not confer with her openly. He was sure they were being spied on. In fact, that might be the reason they had been put together: so the Standards could watch and listen and learn enough to pinpoint the location and plans of the other two. Any plan he and Meilan might make would be balked before it got started, and though their captivity had been gentle enough so far, any misbehavior could change that radically. And he couldn't even climb or run well. Not with his tender ankle.

But it was a challenge of a sort: How could they plan anything, let alone execute it, under constant observation? Suddenly he had an inspiration.

When the diner closed and the supply room opened, John wasted no time. "I'd like a typewriter," he said to the communicator.

"Please define," the machine voice said. John defined.

"There is no such instrument in stock."

He was not surprised. Probably his own typewriter, back at the Caucasian enclave, had been specifically reconstituted from ancient specifications for his benefit. He had suspected that typewriters were no longer used by man. In fact, it was possible that *writing* was no longer used by man. Why should it be, when communicators could talk intelligently and viewscreens brought a comprehensive slate of programs to every octagonal cubbyhole? He and Betsy might be the only literate people on the planet. And Pei and Meilan—only they would write Chinese, not English.

Then another realization struck him full-blown. English, Chinese, and whatever language they spoke in Songhai. Different languages entirely, with no common root for at least ten thousand years. He should not be able to understand Meilan or Ala at all, for he knew only his own language. But he *did* understand them, and they understood him, and each other. *They all spoke the same language— Standard.*

Actually, it made sense. It would have made the zoo-keeping chore terrifically complicated if every bit player of every enclave had to learn a foreign language and speak it without accent. And how were the zoo specimens to know the difference? He *thought* he spoke English, and Meilan probably thought she spoke Chinese, and so on.

But the Newton library of books—had they all been written just for him? That seemed overly complicated, too. Some of them were very old books, with special bindings—hard to forge in a hurry. Yet they matched his language. The phonic rules, the haphazard spelling that defied all logic— that had to be the product of linguistic evolution, not a modern invention. So the Standards *did* have a written language. Or did the Standards actually speak English? That would account for the books matching. But then how about Meilan's written language? Chinese symbols were nothing like the Western alphabet.

Well, he would find out, for his escape plan depended on the written word. Whatever language the Standards spoke, most of them were probably illiterate. Few people ever learned more than they had to.

"So you don't have a typewriter," he said to the communicator, feigning disappointment. "Then how about a keyboard with letters and numbers, set up the same way? It could be plugged into your main circuit, and you could transcribe it for me. Know what I mean?"

"This is possible, if you do not wish to dictate verbally in the normal fashion."

"I *don't* wish. I need my typing practice, and now's an excellent time to get it, instead of twiddling my thumbs. Someday I may get my real typewriter back."

Did that imply that the things of the enclave were

more real than those of the outside world? He'd have to watch that sort of thinking!

A few minutes later there was a *thunk!* in the supply room. A keyboard unit was there. It looked like an adding machine, since it had no roller or paper or internal keys, but it would do. John lifted it out and carried it to the table. Meilan was sitting with hands folded, unmoving. "Why don't you lie down if you're tired?" he asked her, knowing she would deny being tired.

"I am not resting. I am contemplating I Ching."

"Who?"

"I Ching. This is a—a philosophy. You would think of it as a book."

"Written in Chinese?"

"In the word-symbols of the Middle Kingdom. But I do not need to read it, for I know the hexagrams."

Distracted for the moment, John questioned her further. "If you know what's in it, why are you worrying about it?"

"There are many intriguing riddles within the hexagrams and many illuminating interpretations."

"That's neat, I'm sure. But what's it *about*?"

"About life. It offers sage advice for every situation. It is a very satisfying manuscript."

That sounded like religion, and he decided to steer clear of that subject for the time being. "Why don't you order a game or something, to pass the time?" he asked her. "We don't know how long we'll be here, and anything we want we have to order now or wait for the next cycle. Come to think of it, I should get a bone for Canute."

"I doubt they have Wei-ki," she said.

"Your philosophy book? I meant, well, like a paper-and-pencil game." And to the communicator: "One rawhide bone, please."

"Wei-ki, not I Ching," she said, smiling.

"Please define," the communicator said at the same time.

"It's a bone-shaped object formed from a section of rawhide for a dog to chew on. It's very stiff and tastes of—well, rawhide. Animal skin."

"It is forbidden to take animal life unnecessarily," the communicator said.

"Oh." He'd forgotten that aspect of Standard society. "Well, an imitation, then. Just so it's tasty and chewy."

"One moment, please."

In that moment he returned to Meilan. "Then what is Wei-ki? A map of Pei's city?"

She smiled again. "It is the game of enclosing. Very old, very good. But I would need a board eighteen squares on a side and two hundred pips of each color. . . ."

"Couldn't you make your own board with paper and pencil?"

"Pencil?"

"You don't know what a *pencil* is?" he asked, amazed. "To write with, to draw."

"Ah. A brush."

"And makeshift pieces. There must be *something*."

She looked at him, a tiny furrow between her eyes. "As you say."

There was another *thunk!* as Canute's delicacy arrived. It was a simulated bone formed from simulated rawhide, but the dog was well satisfied. He busied himself in an obtuse corner, chewing and chewing.

Meilan began explaining to the communicator what supplies she needed to make a Wei-ki set. John doodled on the typing board. THE QUICK BROWN FOX JUMPS OVER THE LAZY DOG, he typed. He didn't need to see it on paper—in fact, didn't want to. Then: COMMUNICATOR: PLEASE PRINT THE FOREGOING MESSAGE.

A slip of paper emerged from a slot in the wall. He pulled it free. He was afraid it would not be intelligible, but it was neatly and correctly printed exactly as he had typed it. Good enough.

He paused to watch Meilan lifting out her supplies. "Here—I'll set up a table for you," he said. He shoved it against the wall by the paper slot and drew the chair up so that it faced away from him. As she took her place, directing another perplexed glance at him, he ambled back to his typer and sat down for more practice.

COMMUNICATOR: PLEASE PRINT THE FOREGOING MESSAGE IN MIDDLE KINGDOM SYMBOLS. Then: IGNORE THE FOLLOWING UNTIL I ADDRESS YOU SPECIFICALLY AGAIN. And he proceeded to type random sentences.

"I have set up the game," Meilan said after a time, "but I have no one with whom to play."

Had she received his devious message? "Is it complicated?"

"For the novice, very. Far easier for a fox to leap over a sleeping hound."

Yes! "Then I'd be no good. I can't even win at checkers." And he typed: COMMUNICATOR: PLEASE PRINT THE FOLLOWING MESSAGE IN MIDDLE KINGDOM SYMBOLS.

"Checkers?"

"An American game. Like chess only less so." MEILAN, WE HAVE TO KEEP THE STANDARDS DISTRACTED. THEY CAN SURELY SEE AND HEAR US, BUT I DON'T THINK THEY REALIZE WHAT WE'RE REALLY DOING. PLAY A MOCK GAME.

"I'll try to play it by myself, then," she said.

"Sorry I couldn't help." THEY MAY THINK THEY'RE OUTSMARTING US, BUT THEY WON'T LEAVE US TOGETHER FOREVER. MY GUESS IS WE'LL BE HELD UNTIL THEY CAPTURE BETSY AND PEI AND MAKE SURE HUMÉ AND ALA ARE CONFINED. THEN THEY'LL SEE TO IT THAT WE NEVER ESCAPE AGAIN. I THINK WE'D BETTER GET OUT WHILE WE CAN. IF WE CAN. WE CAN MAKE PLANS THIS WAY.

"I don't know whether this will work," she said. "It is not a good game when I know what the other side plans."

"It's the same with checkers." I FIGURED OUT HOW WE COULD TALK. CAN YOU FIGURE OUT HOW TO GET OUT OF HERE? LET ME KNOW SOMEHOW.

John stopped, stretched his fingers, stood up, and

walked away from the typer as though bored with his practice. He was afraid to overdo it; too much typing would make the watchers suspicious, and a little suspicion was a most dangerous thing.

"Those coordinate figures—have you discovered their basis?" Meilan inquired, not looking up.

"Coordinates? No. We didn't need to know their framework once we found the taxi could follow them directly." Why had she brought *that* up?

"I like intellectual puzzles. My tutor used to give me difficult riddles to solve. I would like to attempt something like that."

"Oh. Sure." It certainly was no secret now about those figures, since they had used them to spot the enclaves. John took a spare sheet of her paper (it was pseudo-paper, too; the feel was subtly different) and borrowed her brush to write them out:

0544071364
3777767256
0000150055

"Each number we tried took us to a separate place on the globe," he said. "We couldn't have given the taxi any other information, because we didn't have any to give. But they can't be the kind of coordinates *I* know, because they are single numbers, not pairs. You need meridians of longitude and latitude, so you can count off north or south and east or west. But since these obviously work, it must be a pretty good system."

He wasn't certain she understood much of this, since she had been educated in the fashion of eighth-century China, but she seemed interested. "What is distinctive about these numbers?" she asked musingly.

"Distinctive? Far as I know, they're just numbers."

"Few numbers are 'just numbers,' " she said, licking her lips as though tasting something intriguing. "Every number is unique, and every set of numbers, too. We must discover in what ways these are special."

John began to react impatiently, since this type of discussion would hardly enable them to escape. Then he thought of two things: first, that if they did escape, they would need to know how to find their way to the rendezvous without benefit of taxis or other Standard devices, which meant they had to understand the coordinate system in detail. Second, this discussion could be Meilan's cover for some more direct notions on escape methods. The two of them had to seem occupied so that the Standards would be lulled.

"Well, they're all ten digits. So I suppose it means that any spot on the planet can be identified by a number just this large—zero to nine billion. For what that's worth."

"Yes. And they are maintained at ten digits even when they must be filled in with initial zeroes, so their uniformity is no coincidence. So we have one factor—but there must be others."

"You sound like a math teacher! I didn't know the Chinese even used the decimal system!"

She smiled. "Perhaps the original T'ang Jen did not."

"T'ang Jen?"

"Men of T'ang—our description of ourselves. Just as you call yourselves American."

"Oh." Was she gently reminding him that his use of the words "China" and "Chinese" was objectionable? Better watch that.

He studied the numbers. Now that they had been written out, he saw another thing. "They run to repetition. The last two do, anyway. Four sevens in a row, four zeroes in a row. Is that significant?"

"Perhaps. Is there anything else?"

"That's about it. There isn't anything more to fasten on. If we had ten numbers or a hundred. . . ."

"Your comment about the differing systems," she said thoughtfully. "You and I appear to understand the numbers the same way—but can we be sure the Standards do? Suppose their digits have different meaning?"

"Brother! If their five means our three, we'll never get it straight!"

"I was thinking of differing sets. Have you noticed that there is no digit higher than seven?"

Startled, he looked again. "You're right! Betsy noticed that, too, in the taxi. Every number from one to seven, but no eight or nine. Out of thirty numbers, you'd expect at least one of those. That could be coincidence or. . . ."

"Or an octal system."

"Octal?"

"Based on eight numerals, not ten. Zero through seven. That may be the significance of the bunching of zeroes and sevens, for they would be at the extremes. You are not familiar with this?"

"Never heard of it," he said sheepishly. "My barbarian education is showing its seams."

She laughed. "It was not my education that spoke. I noticed that the Standard apartments are octagonal. Possibly, then, their numbers are, too."

She had phrased it delicately, but it struck him that Meilan was uncommonly sharp. "But how do you write eight, nine, or ten? In octal?"

"The same as in decimal. Eight becomes one zero; nine is one one; ten is one two. When you add a zero, you are multiplying by eight instead of ten. One hundred in octal would be sixty-four in decimal—eight squared instead of ten squared. And so on."

"I'll be darned," he said, "You men of T'ang do too know what you're doing. Uh, girls of T'ang, I mean."

"If it *is* octal," she said, absorbed in the problem, "the row of sevens would be very close to the row of zeroes."

"Say, yes! 7777 would be just one digit below 10000. Except that there's a three starting off that second figure and no one leading off the other. So it must be just below 40000 instead."

"That is what interests me. It is as though these numbers ought to be very close, but are not, because of their beginnings and the remainder of the digits. It really is not close at all, and we may be mistaken."

"I'm not so sure." John studied the three long numbers, his head almost touching hers. "Look— the lead-off digits are all low—under four—while the end ones are all higher. Do you think that means anything?" Then before she could reply, he had another flash. "We've forgotten that these are *coordinates*! They have to be double numbers—to show vertical and horizontal. Easting and northing, latitude and longitude, or whatever. Why not two numbers of five each!" His words tumbled over themselves as they almost raced ahead of his thoughts. "Four is the middle of the octal system, isn't it, just as five is the middle of the decimal. So four might be the dividing point. All the longitudes could be numbered below four and all the latitudes above it. And zero could be both your starting point and your finishing point, because we are dealing with a globe. . . ."

Melian's enthusiasm was more restrained. "Why keep the longitudes low and the latitudes high? There is no need——"

"To tell them apart! These numbers are all jumbled together. If one digit were left out accidentally, the whole thing could be fouled up. But if you *know* the low ones have to be——"

She waved her hand as though shooing flies

away. "All right. It is a mighty leap from a thin observation, but let's consider it. We now have three pairs of five-digit numbers." She wrote them out:

05440—71364
37777—67256
00001—50055

"See!" he exclaimed, pointing. "37777 and 00001—just one digit either side of the base line. Those points are close together!"

"Not according to the other coordinates in each pair," she protested. Her brush doodled on another scrap of paper.

"And they *are* close, because we thought we were coming down in Humé's enclave, and instead we hit Ala's!" Then her objection registered. "Oh-oh."

"They could be very close in longitude but far apart in latitude," Meilan said. "Those second figures are 17201 units apart."

Chastened, he considered. "Depends on how much territory each number covers. Maybe we could work it out on a model globe." He looked about but saw nothing that would do. He had lost his impetus, however; seventeen thousand units had to be large, however they translated.

Meilan had been making what appeared to be casual doodles on her sheet of paper as they talked. Now she folded it, then folded it again, her hands working busily. Soon she had an intricately fashioned paper ball—not crumpled but smooth. "Will this do?"

John took it with less enthusiasm than he might have had and sketched light lines around it, careful not to crush or penetrate the paper with the brush. He circled the sphere completely, then circled it again at right angles. "Like quartering an orange," he remarked and realized that he could have ordered an orange from supply or (in case that counted as food and so had to wait for the kitchen compartment) a ball or even a globe itself. "But our globe has a hole at the north pole."

"Look inside. You might see something interesting."

"Like maybe the molten core of the earth!" Laughing, he put his eye to the hole.

Inside, on the opposite side of the ball, was her sketch of his typer. "Ask it," she murmured almost inaudibly.

He looked up. "What?"

"But you have made only two lines on the surface," she said.

He had thought of them as four but decided they were indeed only two, each circling the globe completely. So he made two more circles converging at the same point. "North and south pole."

She looked at him, startled by a memory. "Once I heard—I thought it was nonsense—something about the west pole."

"The *west* pole!"

"The north and west poles. I'm sure, now. The two of them. I listened at night when the Standards thought I slept, and heard—that is all I remember."

"How can there be a *west* pole!" he demanded.

She smiled and pointed to the paper globe. "Here."

"On the *equator*? That's ridiculous!"

She took the globe and brush and began to fill in the westing meridians. Two of the circles duplicated those already established: the equator and one of the four great circles. The other two cut obliquely across these.

"In here," Meilan said, tapping the globe, "is the answer. If you ask."

At that moment the supply cubicle closed off, and the hall cubicle opened, startling them. For an instant he thought they might escape through it but quickly saw that it was an empty shaft with slick walls. They had to have the elevator, and there seemed to be none.

Meilan went up and looked in. "There is a barrier," she said, tapping it. So there was, a transparent panel. The Standards had not over-looked so obvious a weakness in their prison. Or maybe it was the regular protection against falling into the shaft, which could be fogged with an ID key.

John returned to the globe and studied the effect of Meilan's added lines, mildly fascinated. The interlocking networks were regular in themselves but formed irregular shapes. Some were triangles,

some trapezoids. A number of angles were right—
ninety degrees—but more were acute and some
obtuse. "I would get seasick using these coordinates," he remarked. Yet it made a kind of sense,
for no north or south, east or west, had to be
differentiated. These two sets would do the job.

"If the planet matches earth in size," Meilan
said, "each of those lines sets off an eighth of it,
so——"

"How do you know so much?" he demanded
with surprised admiration. "Back in your time
people didn't even know the world was round, and
here you are talking about planets!"

"I listened more than was proper," she admitted
demurely.

"And I never even caught on to the Standards
until last year!" He returned to the problem of the
globe. "An eighth of it for each line, you say. That
would be three thousand miles, about. But those are
only the major divisions. Our coordinates have five
digits. They must divide it up—how small would
that be, in the octal system? I can't visualize it."

"Let me make an abacus." She arranged her
game tokens in several columns, like a series of
dotted *i*'s. Each shaft consisted of five pips, with the
single-pip dot a couple of spaces above. She had
nine such columns. Then she began moving the
pips back and forth, so that some of the dots came
down to join part of the stems, and the columns
became new formations of three and three, two and

four, or even a solid six. John did not speak, for she was obviously concentrating.

"Down to less than one of your miles," she said at last.

"Then that's it! Those five-digit pairs can pin-point any spot on the planet within a mile." He turned the model about, marking in numbers. "And look! If a point is on that zero line, it has to be at the west pole, the way I've marked it, because that's the only place you can get an intersection."

"That should not be so," she said. "They would not make wasteful coordinates."

He shrugged. "Let's plot our three coordinates and see how it works. How much do you want to bet that Humé and Ala are only a couple of miles apart?"

It worked—except for one thing. There were two locations for every coordinate. They were directly opposite each other, across the globe, twelve thousand miles apart, traveling around the out-side—as was necessary for human purposes. They could discover no way to tell which one was correct—assuming that their laboriously worked-out system was in order.

John sighed. Well, it had been only a game. Or *had* it?

Meilan seemed disappointed, too. It was as though she had expected more from him. The way she had tapped the globe, telling him rhetorically that the answer was in it. Actually there was only her sketch of his typer inside. Meanwhile the hall door gaped temptingly, proffering illusory escape, and valuable time was passing.

His eye fell on the typer, the real one, and abruptly he knew what she had been trying to suggest to him. Subtly, so that the Standards would not catch on. So subtly that he had missed her cues himself, and yet so obvious that he had been blind not to have realized it instantly. No wonder Meilan had been disappointed with him. Escape was ridiculously simple—maybe.

10

Rescue
and Reunion

COMMUNICATOR: PLEASE ANSWER THE FOLLOWING
THEORETICAL QUESTION IN T'ANG SYMBOLS. HOW
CAN TWO PUREBRED PEOPLE AND A GOMDOG ESCAPE
CONFINEMENT IN A TYPICAL STANDARD APARTMENT?

Meilan read the answer. Her shoulders began
shaking. John rushed over to her, uncertain whether
she was laughing, crying, or choking. It seemed to
be all three. He started to ask her about the
communicator's message, then caught himself. It
would be folly to discuss it out loud; that was the
whole point in using the typer and symbols. But
what was so emotional about the matter?

After a moment she stood up, pulled open the
drawer in the table they had been using, put her
hand inside, and removed something. Nonchalantly
she passed it into his hand. It was an ID key.

John looked at the desk with dismay. The key had been there all the time! They had never thought to look. Now they had only to take it and phase open the hall barrier and ride right out of the building. . . .

Meilan held him back gently, shaking her head no.

No? But then he understood. Naturally there would be an alarm of some sort the moment they entered the hall. The Standards might have forgotten to clean out the drawer, but they were not *that* careless. But what, then, was the communicator's plan?

"Tell it to execute," she murmured, nodding toward the typer. "Then sleep for an hour."

Baffled, he went to the typer. COMMUNICATOR: PLEASE EXECUTE YOUR PLAN.

Nothing happened.

He drew down a bunk from one of the nonopening walls and lay down, feigning sleep. He had almost missed his cue before, not realizing that Meilan was trying to suggest that he type his query on the communicator. This time he meant to play out the game without a hitch, even though it made no present sense to him.

Meilan lay down on another bunk. He was sure she wasn't really asleep, either. For an hour they lay silently. The hall closed, and the bathroom opened again, but they "slept" through this, too. Canute had no trouble: His snooze was genuine.

When the hour was over (it had seemed like

two!), Meilan got up and came to wake him. "The lavatory will be closed soon," she said with maidenly hesitation.

Still ignorant of the meaning of all this, he entered the bathroom with Canute. But as they tried to leave a few minutes later, Meilan stopped him. Silently she guided John back into the main section, where he had regained consciousness amid the foam. She had him lie down on the rough slanted floor. She lay down, too, and Canute was happy to join the fun. There was barely room for them all.

There was a warning light together with a tone as the bathroom hour neared its end. (Actually, he wasn't sure how close to an hour it was, but it was easiest to call it that.) They had about two minutes to vacate, but they did not move. As time ran out, he caught on. How simple!

The apertures shifted. The wall to the right of their original entrance opened. The bathroom was now facing onto a new apartment. Meilan led him into it. John saw that this was number twenty-two—eighteen in decimal reckoning. They were still in the heart of the building but out of view of the monitors—with luck.

"Now we wait an hour," Meilan murmured.

"Won't they miss us in thirty-two?"

"The communicator is projecting a solid image of us sleeping. They won't know we're gone."

So that was what happened after he typed EXECUTE! A camera had photographed a posed sequence for playback after they left. Very neat.

"Suppose the owner of this apartment comes back and finds us?"

"It is unoccupied, and we shall use the hall before any other person can come. The communicator knows about such things. It says there is no alarm in this hall, so we can just walk out. There will be a taxi waiting above."

John shook his head. "This is too simple. There's a catch."

She looked at her paper. Middle Kingdom symbols were printed in tight vertical rows on it. "It says it will modify the plan if anything happens."

"Remember what Pei said—the machine should serve its master. How do we know it's on *our* side?"

She shrugged. "We asked for advice. It gave it."

John wasn't satisfied, but there did not seem to be much of a choice, particularly at this point. Either they followed the printed instructions or they didn't. They had to trust the communicator and assume that if it were not exactly on their side, it was at least indifferent. A machine did not care who operated it, and this was a type of computer.

Yet what about Pei and Betsy? If they had been captured, there would be nowhere for him and Meilan to go. If the others remained free, how could they be found? In fact, this whole easy escape smacked of a Standard device to locate the other escapees. The Standards had tried watching the prisoners, and it hadn't worked, so now there was this. The moment the purebreds rejoined, the jaws of the trap would clamp on them all. But it would not be safe to voice his suspicions to Meilan. He could never foil the Standards that way, for if he were correct, they would still be listening.

He borrowed Meilan's brush and checked to see whether it retained any fluid. He discovered that it was actually a kind of pen, feeding ink into the bristles without dripping. He turned over his coordinates sheet and began sketching octagons.

By the time the hall to number twenty-two opened John had a pretty good idea of the layout of the building. Their thirty-two was surrounded by twenty-one, twenty-two, forty-one, and forty-two in the octal system. This twenty-two was surrounded by twelve, thirteen, thirty-two, and thirty-three. And they were on the fourth floor; he had spotted a plaque identifying it. Now, if he could just discover the coordinates of this building—the true coordinates, not what the Standard communicator might tell them. . . .

But the elevator had arrived. It occurred to John that a power failure in a residence like this would be a very serious matter: no light, no food, and no escape. Probably no air, either, for long.

That got him to wondering just what the power source was. Electricity could account for the appurtenances, but where and how was it generated? He had seen no smokestacks or power lines. And the taxi—nothing he knew of could explain its operation. It had no propeller and no jets, yet it flew.

Meilan nudged him, and he saw that the elevator was beginning to move on. They phased through the panel with the new ID and jumped aboard. Evidently the Standards gave no person more than his share of time for anything!

Then John acted. He touched the button that put the elevator on manual control, overriding its prior directive. Then he guided it down, not up. Meilan stared at him but did not speak.

They halted at the basement. John's hand was shaking as he phased through the gate, but they were in luck: The chamber beyond was empty. A long, level hall stretched away in both directions.

"Find a way out!" John told Canute.

The dog dashed down one hall, sniffing at cross passages. They followed him, passing elevator doors every few feet. John realized that every one of the twenty or more shafts opened at this level, serving over five hundred apartments. It was possible to get to any room in the building from here, but by the same token it was possible for anyone to discover them here. *Hurry*, he thought.

Then Canute turned off, and there was a flight of conventional stairs. They climbed these and found themselves at street level.

But of course there was no street. There was only a forest.

"You had reason?" Meilan inquired once they were out of sight of the building. There was no sarcasm in her voice, just the question. There would have been a real scene with Betsy, but Meilan was smarter and more obliging. Fortunately.

John explained why he had broken up the communicator's plan. "Maybe it was honest, and maybe it was a trap," he finished. "But this way, we *did* escape."

"They could watch us as well among the trees as in a sphere."

"I don't think so. This isn't an enclave. I think they were overconfident, sure that their plan was working. When we changed course, we dropped out of the net. They may not know what happened."

She considered for a moment. "I agree," she said, surprising and pleasing him. He had expected more of an argument.

"Now we have to figure out where our friends are and how to reach them. I didn't plan beyond this point. In fact, I wasn't sure there really was forest land out here; it might have been artificial."

Canute woofed.

"Oh-oh," John said. "That's his 'chase' warning. Someone's after us."

Now they could hear the hum of a ground-sphere. "Perhaps a routine mission?" Meilan asked hopefully.

The hum grew louder. They had had one encounter with a ground-sphere and its paralyzing beams. It would be foolish to risk that again.

"What can we do?" Meilan whispered.

John looked about but saw nothing but trees. If the sphere were following them, it would find them anywhere they ran. His ankle twinged reminiscently; no sense hurting it again by ludicrous heroics. Their position was hopeless.

"Ask your I Ching," he said, taking his bitterness out on her.

To his amazement and disgust, she concurred. "Yes. We should have done that before we started. I will consult I Ching."

John judged by the sounds that the pursuit was within a quarter mile, and he knew the small spheres could move at at least thirty miles per hour. That meant about thirty seconds until capture. He did not want it to end so ludicrously. "Meilan, I was joking—not that it makes any difference."

"But I have no yarrow sticks!" she cried, oblivious to his words. "I know the hexagrams, but the selection must be random."

"Flip a coin," he said with resignation. To have come so close to escape, and now to wait so helplessly!

"I have none!" she cried.

He saw that she was really upset. Probably it was transference from the tension of the chase—being emotional about something inconsequential. Sometimes it had happened to him, too. "I have a penny—an American coin," he said and presented it to her.

She snatched it from him. "I will call the head divided," she said. "The building undivided."

"What are you talking about?" The pursuit hum was louder, but evidently he had overestimated the sphere's speed.

Meilan ignored him. "One throw per line. It is not proper, but we have too little time." She spun the coin to the ground. "Six, divided."

She scraped a place bare of leaves, then drew a broken line in the dirt. She threw the coin again. "Six, divided."

"Still heads. Where do you get this 'six' business?"

She drew a second broken line parallel to the first, above it. She threw again. "Six, divided."

The hum of the sphere was becoming so loud he was sure the thing would burst upon them in an instant. In fact, it sounded like several spheres this time.

"Six, divided," she announced again, drawing a fourth pair of lines above the others. "Six, divided. And six, divided."

"Broken record," he muttered. "You can't be flipping properly; it always comes up heads."

But her figure was complete: two columns of parallel lines.

—— ——
—— ——
—— ——
—— ——
—— ——
—— ——

"That is—let me think—that is the khwan hexagram. The earth mother—the symbol of submission."

The spheres still had not come into sight. Now John was sure this was deliberate. By the sounds, he and Meilan were being encircled. There was no possible escape. "Submission, yes," he murmured. "It's right about that. We have no choice. But still I'd like to——"

"The superior man must not take the initiative," she said firmly. "That is the message of I Ching. We must wait."

"Fat lot of good that advice does us now! I don't need any Ching to tell me we're sunk. What do we do after we're caught and locked up? Does it tell you that?"

"I Ching tells everything. I will make another hexagram. For you, Smith John, so that you will know what you must do—when that time comes."

John started to make a sarcastic reply but caught himself. She wasn't joking! She believed in this I Ching and in her distraction had even put his name backward in Chinese fashion. "All right. But be careful how you flip that coin. It's no good if it isn't random, is it?"

"I did say random, but it is not. The circumstance of the supplicant guides the hexagram; otherwise the advice I Ching offers would not be valid. But it is not for me to influence the turn of the coin." She flipped it again, more carefully. "This is the first nine, undivided." She drew a single long line and flipped again. "The second six, divided."

After that there were two more tails: nines, undivided. John watched with growing interest, but at the same time he was increasingly nagged by the silence around them. The spheres had encircled them and stopped. What did it mean?

Finally a head and a tail: six, divided, and nine, undivided. He was catching on to the system. The finished diagram differed from the first:

$$
\begin{array}{cc}
\rule{3cm}{0.5pt} \\[2pt]
\rule{1.2cm}{0.5pt} \quad \rule{1.2cm}{0.5pt} \\[2pt]
\rule{3cm}{0.5pt} \\[2pt]
\rule{3cm}{0.5pt} \\[2pt]
\rule{1.2cm}{0.5pt} \quad \rule{1.2cm}{0.5pt} \\[2pt]
\rule{3cm}{0.5pt}
\end{array}
$$

"Li," Meilan said. "The hexagram of clinging, brightness, fire, light. The symbol of adherence and intelligence."

"Intelligence." John knew it was foolish to be flattered by the verdict of a series of coin flips, but he was. "What does it say to do?"

"The intelligent man will adhere strictly to what is correct."

"But what is correct?" he cried. "To wait here, doing nothing? To—to take no initiative?"

"Perhaps. I Ching does not foretell the future. It guides one to proper attitudes and decisions."

"Maybe so. But we're about to be taken prisoner again. The Standards are all around us, probably listening right now. And this time we won't get away. You can bet on that. We have to act *now*—if we're ever going to."

She was adamant. "I Ching is never mistaken. We must take no initiative. We must adhere to what is correct."

"Make another hexagram. I want a recount." But he knew it was already way too late to do anything, even if he had anything in mind to do. Whatever time they might have had, had been frittered away by this supernatural inanity.

Gravely, Meilan lifted the coin.

"Let me do that," he said, taking it from her. Better this than nothing!

His first flip was tails. "First nine, undivided," he said, drawing a single line.

As he prepared for the second throw, he saw them: uniformed Standards converging. Some carried objects that might be weapons. John pretended not to be aware of them. Meilan had said no initiative; okay, he would take none. He warned Canute with a quick gesture.

He flipped. "Second six, divided." He drew it.

The Standards came to stand in a loose circle around the three of them. The visitors did not speak.

John flipped again. "Third six, divided." Weren't the Standards going to *do* anything?

"Fourth six, divided. Fifth nine, undivided. Sixth nine, undivided." He completed the hexagram.

———————
———————
——— ———
——— ———
——— ———
———————

"Yi," Meilan said. "The symbol of increase, of addition. This man will overcome the greatest difficulties and gain advantage."

John stood up. "That," he said with ironic satisfaction, "is more like it."

"Come with us, please," one of the Standards said.

The games were over. John and Meilan walked with the Standards, and Canute followed docilely.

There was a noise like thunder cracking overhead, and a sudden stiff wind struck them. "Thunder and wind, too!" Meilan cried, her face animated. "That is part of yi!"

Then the Standards fell away on either side. John and Meilan and Canute were the only ones to remain standing. A sphere descended suddenly.

"Don't just gawk! Jump in!"

It was Betsy. Rescue was at hand.

11

Guerrilla
Tactics

For a moment it was another scramble, as John and Meilan climbed into the taxi and hung on while acceleration tore at their bodies. John kept one hand at Canute's collar, preventing the dog from sliding back out the fogged door while the craft ascended. Then things steadied. John sat up and saw Ala.

He lurched to his feet, crossed the small floor, and kissed her. He turned to face Betsy and Meilan. They were no more amazed than he.

"Just what have you been up to?" Betsy demanded.

John had no answer. What he chiefly remembered about Ala was her golden ornament. And one other thing: "What did you mean—'The palm leaf despises the hippo'?"

She smiled. "It was a spell to ward off attack."

"A spell. Do you believe in magic?"

"I do. And it had its effect until you used the counterspell."

"I did no such thing!"

Ala only smiled again.

Meilan said: "I have already met Humé, and of course John and Betsy and Pei. But not Ala, except by reputation."

Ala nodded. "Humé told me of you. I think he prefers the Middle Kingdom to Songhai."

Humé, who had been expertly guiding the taxi until now, turned to face John. "Just as Ala prefers America to Kanem/Bornu." He was black and handsome and large. "Did Meilan importune you also with her infidel book?"

"Did she! We were casting hexagrams while the Standards stood and watched over our shoulders. And you know—those I Chings were right! First one said to stand pat. Second said to do what was correct. Third said we would win out. And then you rescued us, so it all came true, coincidentally."

"Coincidentally!" Betsy exclaimed indignantly. "Why didn't you follow the original plan? We were waiting to pick you up on the rooftop. Then you didn't show, and we thought we'd been tricked."

"*You* were waiting? The communicator arranged that?"

"We received a cryptic message. It seemed to be from you. From Meilan, rather, because it was in Chinese symbols only Pei could read. So we took a chance and came. Then you——"

"So the I Ching was right again!" John said, bemused. "It was my initiative that messed it up. I thought it was a trap. I guess I did the wrong thing."

"You generally do," Betsy said.

"It does not matter," Humé said. "It is more important that we decide what to do now."

"Humé knocked out those Standards with their own rays," Betsy said warmly. "He knows all about weapons."

"We must decide," Humé said, "or be captive again."

"I think not," Pei said.

"Listen to him," Betsy said. "He's a scholar."

John noticed that there was no sarcasm in her voice when she spoke of Yao Pei. She was impressed with him, all right.

"I do not believe the Standards tried very hard to make us captive," Pei said. "They may believe that we will return to our own enclaves if given leisure to do so."

"Return!" John exclaimed. "Why?"

"Because the enclaves are familiar, and the Standard world is not. We can have everything we need inside, whereas outside we are comparative savages."

"Better a savage than a zoo specimen!" John said.

Pei shrugged.

"You know," Betsy said thoughtfully, "my parakeet seemed to be happiest in the cage. Outside it could bang into windowpanes or land on a hot pot. Once it tried to take a bath in a cup of cocoa."

"We are not parakeets," Humé said.

"Can we really have everything we need?" Ala inquired, glancing at John.

Nobody answered. On the physical level the answer was yes. On the emotional level, involving personal concepts of freedom, self-respect, and romance, it was no.

"We cannot fly along forever," Humé said. "We do not know how to find our way by ourselves."

"We can find our way," John said. "Meilan and I worked out the Standard coordinates system, pretty much."

"Excellent! But we still must act together. We should choose a leader."

"Yes," John said. "Who?"

There was an awkward silence.

Ala was first to tackle the problem. "It should be a male."

Meilan agreed immediately. Betsy hesitated, then nodded. "But which one?"

John wanted to be the leader, but he was also afraid of the responsibility. His hands were sweating. Neither Humé nor Pei looked any more at ease. How was this diverse group to make the choice?

"Since the ladies have renounced the position," Pei said, "perhaps they should make the selection."

John exchanged glances with Humé, startled by the simplicity of this suggestion. The three girls looked at each other, just as surprised. "Well, why not?" Betsy demanded as though someone were debating it. Her forwardness contrasted with the reticence of the others.

The taxi was crowded with the six of them and Canute, and there was no place for the girls to talk privately. Betsy pulled the others down so that their heads were together. There was an animated whispering, and twice all three girls tittered.

At length they stood up. "We decided to do this scientifically," Betsy announced. "You'll draw straws." She held up her fist, showing three bits of ribbon. "The long one gets it." She came at John, proffering the display.

"Hurry up, John," Betsy said.

Irritated, he yanked out a length of yellow ribbon. It was about three inches long. Was that long or short? Did he *want* it long—or short?

Humé was next. Smiling, he took a piece of black ribbon. It seemed to be about the same length as John's. Pei accepted a white ribbon, having no choice. It was twice the length of the others.

"Very well," Pei said, assuming command as though the issue had never been in doubt. "Humé, you are competent in weapons and logistics and military tactics. Do you also know how to handle an interplanetary craft?"

"I studied to be a warrior," Humé said. "I can lead a party safely over rough ground, avoiding ambushes, and I can navigate small boats—or boatlike vehicles such as this one—but I did not

know what a planet was until you told me some
hours ago. A military man learns not to operate
outside his competence."

Pei nodded. "John, you have a general education, but your period is the most modern of our
three. Could you handle such a craft?"

"I used to dream of being a spaceship captain,"
John admitted. "I read about *Sputnik* and the orbital
flights and really went wild. And of course I've
liked science fiction right along. Standard technology—well, it would be suicidal to mess with one of
their spaceships. You'd need a super computer just
to set course, and I don't know anything about
computers."

"Would they resemble the communicators we
have used?"

John's mouth fell open. "Yes! If a spaceship
were keyed in to one of those units, it could do
anything! You'd still have to watch for acceleration
and free fall and incorrect orbit. . . ."

"Yes," Pei said. "I shall be our leader—until we
prepare to enter space. Then John——"

"Space!" Betsy exclaimed. "What——"

"Will assume command, for he comprehends
those problems best," Pei continued without a
break. "When we arrive at earth——"

"Earth!"

"Not knowing what we will find, Humé will be
our leader, for we may have to fight."

He paused now, but no one had any argument.

Pei had evolved a beautiful compromise and an ambitious plan, and they all knew it.

Pei reached out and took Meilan's brush. As he spoke, he made Middle Kingdom doodles on the floor. "Consider a hypothetical case, a contest in which one side has many people, much equipment, and copious information. The other side has few people, poor equipment, and limited knowledge. Yet it must do battle no matter how small its resources. How would it best set about it?"

"Hide and strike," Humé said. "When Kanem was new. . . ."

"Yes, guerrilla warfare," John agreed.

Pei nodded, continuing to write on the floor. "The Hsiung-nu and T'u Chüeh—the barbarian horse-nomads of the western and northern reaches—have employed similar tactics with excellent success. But let us suppose the case is more exaggerated. Perhaps only five or six individuals against an entire planet—and what they say to each other is overheard by the spies of the other side. How might the smaller group prevail?"

John looked at the communicator, startled. Now he saw what Pei was driving at—maybe. Of course the Standards could still be listening! They wouldn't try to close in on the taxi again, but they didn't have to. Every time the purebreds seemed to have escaped a trap, they found a larger one, its jaws closing inexorably. They could not plan anything effective in range of that ever-present Standard ear.

"The smaller group might do best to surrender," Humé said, "and hope for a better opportunity at another time."

Pei nodded no. "Yes."

What? They had already agreed *not* to surrender! And Pei's expression indicated he was ready to fight, yet his words were the opposite.

"Sometimes it is possible to use a man's own power against him," Pei went on.

"Judo," John said. "He charges; you duck and throw him over your back. But I don't see how——"

"You are correct, of course," Pei said, tapping the communicator panel meaningfully. "When the disparity between opposing forces is too great, there can be no contest. The smaller group can only hurt itself by resisting."

Pei had something in mind, obviously, and not what he was saying. He was speaking for the benefit of the eavesdroppers, leading them astray. Yet the chance of success *was* pretty small, in the long run.

"Maybe the Standards are just waiting for us to come to our senses," John said, playing along now. "Less risky."

Meilan came to him. "The writing on the floor—Pei has a plan," she whispered. "What you called guerrilla. But not on land, not physical. On the communicator, in a landscape we cannot see. Yet we can hide in it by making false pictures with words—all together—while we go to the spaceship.

Each must decide what to say, without them knowing."

Then John understood. Modern civilization could not exist without communications, and Pei had grasped that from the perspective of his many-centuries removal from the contemporary scene. If they could somehow obstruct the Standard communications network, there would be chaos, and in that anarchy they very well might take over a spaceship and escape. But how? Overall strategy was one thing; the mundane details were another.

"Pei trusts you know magic words. How to use the strength of their communications system against them," Meilan whispered.

Brother! Now it was up to him again! How *could* they change anything? Nothing a person might say over the phone would knock out the instrument itself! Machines weren't emotional; they did not make judgments; they didn't react. Not *that* way. About all a person could do was tie up the line so that no one else could call the number, making people mad.

John snapped his fingers. Of course! "Call in false reports of our whereabouts," he whispered to Meilan. "And other 'false pictures.' Many of them can be true statements but irrelevant. Irrelevancy still takes up time and channels. Just so the airways are flooded with reports that the authorities have to pay attention to, so that when the *real* report comes in, it can't be distinguished from the others. Meanwhile don't use the communicator for our own journey; keep it on manual. Do we have coordinates for a space port?"

"Humé has many coordinates. I do not know how he found them," she said as she moved back toward Pei.

Routine conversation continued for a few minutes, and the whisperings continued. Then there was a silence. John saw Betsy making notes and did the same himself. They each needed an arsenal of irrelevancy.

Finally Pei looked around. The others nodded.

"Attention," Pei said as he signaled Humé to change course on manual. "T'u Chüeh raiding parties have been sighted on the border. Please address me to the chief of operations."

There was momentary static as a connection was made. "Please repeat the message," a man's voice said.

Pei smiled grimly. "The Huns are invading! Notify the prefect! All troops must be massed for action!"

"Your message is not clear. *Who* is——"

"Huns. Aliens. The barbarian enemy. It is almost too late!"

"Aliens! One moment while I connect you with the Department of Extraplanetary Affairs."

John had an inspiration. "Communicator! How many calls can you handle simultaneously?"

"Four channels are available on this unit."

"Good. Number them one through four. We shall call off the numbers of the ones we wish to use."

Betsy caught on at once. "Channel Two. Attention, all units within the range of this broadcast. There is a dangerous leakage in your primary power supply. Please shut it down until the condition can be corrected. Thank you."

"Channel Three," Ala said. "The palm leaf despises the hippo."

"Channel Three, your message is unclear," a male voice said. "To whom is it addressed?"

"To those who wish to know how to kill the Zin."

"The Zin? Is that an animal? Killing is not permitted. . . ."

"I will narrate the history, since you inquire."

"A simple definition will suffice. The bands are crowded. . . ."

"The river spirit of the great Niger bend was called Zin-kibaru, and he had much magic and music and ruled over the fishes and animals of the water. But there was also a man named Faran whose rice fields were beside the river, and every night Zin-kibaru played his music there and brought the fish to eat Faran's rice. One day Faran went fishing. . . ."

"The airways are very busy. Please define your term more concisely."

John had been ready to start in on Channel Four but couldn't help listening to this peculiar tale. The art of storytelling had been more advanced in bygone centuries!

". . . and only caught two hippopotamuses. He

was angered by this tiny catch—hardly enough to feed his mother and himself for supper—and decided to go fight Zin-kibaru, the water dragon. They met on an island, and Faran demanded Zin's music. 'We shall fight for it,' Zin said, 'but if I win, I will take your canoe.' Faran was little and fat, while Zin was tall and thin. But Faran was winning when Zin uttered this spell: 'The palm leaf despises the hippo.' Faran fell and lost his canoe."

Suddenly John made a connection. That was the spell Ala had used on him!

"So Faran went home, ashamed. 'You are stupid,' said his mother. 'You did not use the counterspell.' Then Faran took another canoe and went after Zin-kibaru again. Faran was winning, and the Zin fled. When Faran caught up, Zin-kibaru said, 'The palm leaf despises the hippo.' But Faran replied, 'If the sun strikes it, what happens to the palm leaf?' And the Zin fell to the ground. So Faran conquered the dragon and gained much power."

John couldn't pause to savor the information. "Channel Four," he said. "Relay this message to the coast guard through a random channel. As follows: Party of six purebreds observed at coordinates 2121056789, leaving a stolen taxi. Emergency."

Meilan nudged him. "Oh-oh," he said. "Correction, Channel Four: Last two digits are one two." He had forgotten the octal system—a giveaway!

"Channel Two," Betsy said. "Uh, route that through a random system." She had caught on to

John's idea: If the call really went through a randomly selected line, it would be difficult or impossible to trace. "Office of the President: A malfunction has been traced to your personal communications set. You are in danger from radiation. Please shut down your set immediately and summon a repair crew."

Humé was guiding the taxi on manual, and there was no sign of pursuit. Was this verbal smoke screen working? They wouldn't know until they landed. It was quite a group effort, though! John listened to the babel of voices for a moment. Pei was telling Channel One another Middle Kingdom tale, evidently taking his cue from Ala. Meilan was on Channel Two now, explaining the psychology of I Ching and instructing the party at the other end in finding a hexagram. Betsy had moved over to Channel Three.

"Route this message randomly to all astronomers," Betsy was saying. "Think of a number. Add fifteen. Subtract four. Delete the number you started with. Multiply the result by two. The number you now have is twenty-two. Remember it, and spread the word."

"That won't work," John warned her. "Remember, their numbering system is octal."

"It is? Communicator, what is my correct answer, then?"

"Twenty-two," the voice replied.

John was taken aback. "But it *can't* be. Not unless. . . ."

Pei broke off from his narration. "Twenty-two in octal would be read eighteen in decimal," he said. "She's not dealing with the numbers she supposes, but the device remains effective."

Betsy said nothing, not wanting to contradict Pei. John was confused, too. How could they tell what system the Standards used if the figures seemed the same?

Well, back to work!

"Channel Four: Route this message randomly to all taxi supervisors, labeled *Urgent!* 'Peter Piper picked a peck of pickled peppers.'" He ran through the rest of it. Then: "Request an immediate response from all taxi passengers, and make note how many answer the question correctly. Turn in the data to the head of the farm bureau for analysis."

Yes, they were guerrillas of communications, hiding behind a barrage of nonsense! It shouldn't work; it *couldn't* work; but Humé kept piloting, and there was no challenge from the Standards.

"One man went to mow!" John sang joyfully, "went to mow the meadow! One man and his dog. . . ." For he spied a complex that very much resembled a space port, and they were gliding toward what had to be a spaceship angled for takeoff.

12

Spacejack

"Keep broadcasting!" Pei warned as the taxi angled in.

Humé knew what he was doing. The taxi never touched ground. It halted just short of the ship and eased in toward the main lock. Then it touched, and the ports of vehicle and ship phased together.

"Move in and take over, Captain," Pei said, grinning.

More nervous than he would admit, John used his ID to open the panel. He stepped through. Canute plunged through beside him, and suddenly John felt better. Any danger was diminished by the presence of the dog.

The ship was much larger than the taxi, but no space was wasted in hallways or antechambers. He stood in the main travel compartment, from the look of it. Two Standards reclined in stress couches, listening to a communications broadcast. They were absorbed with the message and did not notice John immediately.

". . . the eyes, the head, the hands, the feet, and all the other members," a female voice was saying. "Then the Creator set them all in a beautiful garden, where each might live in comfort, so long as they were liberal in almsgiving and showed hospitality to all strangers."

Oh, no! It was one of Ala's stories!

"This is a take-over," John announced loudly. The two heads turned as he fumbled for a better word. "A piracy. A liberation." Everything sounded ridiculous! "I'm assuming command of this ship."

"Oh, a spacejack," the female Standard said. "Everything happens at once! First the com network is swamped with gibberish so we can't get takeoff clearance, and now this!"

"Yes. A spacejack," John said. The word was new to him, but it seemed to fit the situation nicely.

". . . disguised as a leper and visited the garden. 'Oh, Eyes,' he cried. 'I am dying of this loathsome disease and must have a bed for the night.' But the Eyes were repulsed by his aspect, and drove him away. So he went to the Head, and said . . ."

"Does it have to be right now?" the male Standard demanded with irritation. "We are just starting an orbital vacation. We'd have been gone by now if we'd had our clearance for a nonrisk ascent."

"It has to be now," John said. "This vicious beast is impatient." Canute growled obligingly.

". . . to the Stomach, who was the only one to remember the command of his Creator. Stomach gave the leper food and lodging and treated him kindly . . ."

The woman sighed. "Very well. Sign the regular form."

"Sign the form?" John wasn't certain they realized that he meant to steal their ship, not just borrow it.

"The regular spacejack release," she said. "For the recompense. Put your ID here." She looked at him as though about to remark on his pale color, but courtesy restrained her.

Was this legitimate? Would they really give up the ship at the touch of an ID? Was spacejacking this common? John hesitated.

". . . commanded to attend at his court. 'Why have you disobeyed my instructions?' the Creator said. 'You were supposed to show kindness to all strangers, but when I disguised myself and came among you . . .'"

But what could this ID card do except give away his location? By the time the Standards came in force, the ship would be in orbit.

John touched the ID to the small metallic panel she held out, aware that a unique magnetic imprint had been made. He was now officially a pirate.

The man stood up. "Good luck," he said. "She's a good vessel."

". . . to the Eyes he sent blindness; to the Head, headaches; to the Hands, paralysis; to the Feet, rheumatism; only the Stomach escaped. But the Stomach was very stupid, and pleaded to be allowed to share the burdens of his brethren. So the Creator . . ."

"Might I inquire," the woman said as though she knew this was none of her business, "where you mean to voyage?"

Again, John hesitated.

". . . decreed that all other members of the body should be forever subservient to the Stomach. The Head should think of its comfort, the Eyes must constantly watch for its benefit, the Hands must procure and prepare its food, the Feet must carry it whithersoever it needed to go . . ."

But again, why not? "Stomach," John said. "I mean, earth."

The Standards exchanged glances, then shrugged.

John stuck his head back through the phased port. "All ours!"

Ala looked at him, smiling. "And that is why the Stomach suffers pain and is exposed to many dangers, but still is the most favored part of the body," she said.

Takeoff was automatic once the order had been given. They abruptly shut down the guerrilla barrage, demanded a no-risk ascent, and got it. That meant their route was clear; no other ships would cross their coordinates and elevation until they were through.

John sat in the pilot's seat and watched the gauges intently. All registered in their safe ranges, as he understood them. This was no more difficult than giving the taxi a coordinate . . . fortunately.

There was no blast of vapors as the ship took off. It merely launched smoothly into the sky at an angle. They watched the viewscreen, fascinated, as the ground dropped away to reveal wider and wider expanses of field and forest. This world of Standard was beautiful and unspoiled, whatever else it was not. Bands of cloud came between the ship and the land. It was as though they were sailing through floating islands. Then the cloud cover became complete, and the world was featureless.

There was a lot of atmosphere to traverse. The ship continued to accelerate. The first time John looked at the air-passage guage it registered six hundred knots. Next time it was up to thirteen hundred, and he realized they had passed through the sonic barrier without even a shudder. Then two thousand and on up, steadily and smoothly.

Apparently this was the way of it: an angling up, circling the planet, spiraling out until fully spaceborne. Perhaps it would level off when it achieved a full orbit. This didn't strike John as the most efficient mode of takeoff, but it certainly was easy on the passengers.

"What is your power source?" he asked the communicator.

"Total conversion," the ship's voice replied.

"Total conversion of *what* to *what*?"

"Of matter to energy."

That didn't help much. "How long will it take to get to earth?"

"Variable."

John pondered how best to get the information he wanted without displaying his ignorance. Of course it was only a machine, but he still had his pride. There could be a thousand factors affecting their prospective journey—the relative motions of the two planets, the choice of trajectories, considerations of fuel consumption and timing (although this total conversion implied limitless fuel). No simple schedule was possible.

But he would have to tell the others something. He was the pilot and the present leader of the group; he had to evince confidence. "Can the journey be arranged to finish in—um, let me see—in two weeks? Without harm to ship or passengers or undue danger?"

"It can."

"Good enough. Execute."

That was it. They were on their way to earth.

John was pleased with himself. Much later he would learn that he had little reason to be. He had asked the wrong questions, letting his pride keep him ignorant of the most relevant fact.

* * *

The ship, which had seemed so large at first, became more confining with every passing hour. There were only two staterooms, each designed for two people. The cooking and sanitary facilities were small and hardly private. There was no way to get away from the crowd for any length of time. John decreed that at least two of them should be on duty at all times. That made the sleeping accommodations sufficient. Actually, one room might do for that, since each person slept only a third of the time. The other stateroom could be reserved for waking activities, and the main travel compartment would be open to everyone all the time.

"Humé and Pei sleep first," he said. "In eight hours Betsy and Meilan get the room. After that. . . ." He paused as the others chuckled, realizing that he boxed himself into the third shift sleeping with Ala, but there was no way to make it come out even. "I'll sleep in the pilot's chair," he said finally.

"Another must pilot while you sleep," Pei pointed out. "Perhaps you can use the second room."

John nodded, disgruntled but seeing no better alternative. He was not being an effective leader if Pei had to bail him out like that, and he smarted. But that was the least of the problems he was to face. They had two weeks of close confinement to endure. It was amazing how rapidly purebred company palled. Personality conflicts began to develop in the first few hours of enforced idleness.

Betsy and Meilan did not get along. While Humé
and Pei slept and John piloted (or pretended to,
since he did not dare meddle with the ship's
automatic program) and Ala occupied herself weaving some kind of basket in the spare stateroom, the
two other girls sat in the main compartment and
chatted. At first John thought it was innocent
conversation, but gradually their voices sharpened,
and the subtle rancor of it became obvious. They
seemed to be jealous of each other, though he
wasn't certain why.

Betsy was a smart, pretty, outspoken, positive
Western girl, usually the first to voice an opinion
and the most resentful of masculine prerogatives.
Meilan was, despite her normally quiet demeanor
and subdued expression, somewhat more feminine
and considerably more intelligent, however. Good
reason for jealousy, actually!

Of course there was Pei. Betsy liked him—that
was obvious. But he was Chinese, and Meilan was
the one intended for him, according to the Standard
Plan. More jealousy!

"Why don't you girls see about something to
eat?" John suggested, mainly to break it up.

And that was disaster, for the mechanisms of the
food dispenser were mysterious and the tastes of the
two girls differed strongly. Betsy wanted to order
hamburgers on rye. Meilan was dismayed. "The
ground body of a cow? This is not food to eat! Such
animals are for work, not butchery."

"Oh?" Betsy said with mock sweetness. "What *do* you eat, in the civilized Middle Kingdom?"

"Fish, fowl, fruit, rice, sometimes pigs, and tea to drink."

"Fruit, rice, and tea! What a lovely meal!" Betsy said sarcastically. "Why don't we ask Ala what she wants?"

"Of course."

They called Ala in. "How would you like a nice fat slice of pig?" Betsy asked her.

Ala was shocked. "Swine? It is forbidden!"

"They like it in China."

Then John saw the snare. Betsy was playing one culture off against another. He was furious, but thought he'd better stay out of it.

They finally settled on coffee, bean curd and melon.

After intermediate hours the first shift ended. Humé and Pei reappeared, and Betsy and Meilan retired without coming to hair-pulling, much to John's relief. Ala continued her basket-weaving in the other room.

The companionship of the men was more congenial, at first. Humé was giving some gruesome but interesting detail on techniques of jungle combat when Ala joined them in the main compartment. She was nude.

John would have been amused at the horrified reaction of the other males, if he had not been so shocked himself. It was not that Ala was bad looking. She wasn't.

No one spoke, however. John realized that they were waiting for him. It was his place, as Captain, to handle the problem. "Put on some clothing," he muttered, his tongue thick.

Ala looked at him. "Why? It is not cold."

He found he had no sensible reason to give her. "Girls are supposed to be dressed, that's all."

"Not in Songhai. Not unmarried girls, in the heat of the day," she said.

"Songhai is primitive," Humé said. "No good Moslem woman exposes herself. At Kanem we would never tolerate—"

"Oh, who cares about Kanem!" she cried. "You hypocrites, you try to suppress the tribal gods!"

"We're *civilized*!" Humé shouted back. "There is no god but Allah, and Muhammad is—"

"Songhai was ancient before Muhammad ever existed," she said. "The kings of Mali and Songhai and Kanem only converted for political expedience. They never believed."

"Go and get clothed!" Humé said, furious. "A woman has no place talking of politics and religion."

"Hippo!" she said, leaving.

John turned on Humé. "It was *my* job to send her back. I'm leader now."

Humé shrugged massive shoulders and faced him with an assumed blandness. "Why did you not do so, then?"

"Because you butted in!" But he realized as he spoke that he was being irrational. He was jealous

of Humé the same way Betsy was jealous of
Meilan. When he was a third party he could be
objective; when he was the second party his
emotions got in the way. He resented Humé's
authority over Ala.

"I had understood that you both were Moslem,"
Pei remarked to Humé.

"The royal houses are devout. The villages, the
countryside—" Humé shrugged again. "Belief is
slow to change, and there are many primitives.
Even the king does not attempt to hold completely
to Moslem custom. It isn't expedient."

"So she really believes in nature gods and
things?" John asked, intrigued now.

"No," Ala said, reentering fully robed. "When a
spirit grows too violent, I can tell him the wood he
is made of. But I'm not sanctimonious about Allah,
either."

"Well, we all have different religions, I guess,"
John said. "I'm Christian, and so is Betsy."

"Meilan and I are Confucian," Pei said.
"Though she is also a Buddhist, while I am
Taoist."

"You belong to *two* religions?" John asked,
amazed.

"Certainly. They are complementary, not
exclusive."

"That's ridiculous. You can't worship two
gods!"

"Why not?"

"It just isn't—you *can't*, that's all!" But he felt

his moral footing eroding. These new concepts were disquieting.

"What is there to prevent me? Though of course Confucius is not a god. The principle remains."

"There is no god but Allah," Humé put in.

"No!" John exclaimed.

"*No?*" Humé stood up, looking very much the warrior.

"We must have religious tolerance," Pei said quickly.

"Why?" Humé demanded. "It only leads to a shameless exposure."

Ala looked angry now.

"We can't argue like this," John said. "We have an important mission to accomplish. We have to stick together."

Humé sat down slowly. "That is right. I would not care to begin my hajj in blood."

The respite was brief. Half and hour later Betsy burst into the main compartment in a Standard nightie, hair flouncing. She pointed an accusing finger at John. "Your damned animal! Do you know what he's done?"

Oh-oh. John could smell it now.

"Right on my dress!" she said indignantly.

John could understand her feelings, but had to defend Canute. "We're cooped up on a spaceship. He can't just go outside. So he looked for some newspaper, and if your tunic happened to be folded into a square—"

"If I catch him," she said, "I'll rub his ugly nose in it!"

"Stay away from him!" John said, alarmed. "He knows you don't like him. He's not vicious, but if you touch him—"

"Well, keep him out of my room! Who's going to clean it up?"

"I will," John said. "He's my dog. I won't punish him, though, because I know he was trying to do the right thing."

"Wait till he does it on *your* clothing!"

But John didn't have to clean it up. Humé had already taken care of the matter. Then Ala produced the basket she had been making. "It is for Canute," she said, "for he has no place to sleep except the floor."

"Oh. Thanks," John said, nonplussed. "But I'm not sure—I mean, he never slept in a basket before. He's a big dog—"

"Canute!" she called.

Tail wagging uncertainly, Canute approached. Humé came and lifted him into the basket. Canute was, as John said, a big dog; he weighed well over fifty pounds and did not like to be picked up. But he put up with this without protest, sniffed the basket from inside, turned around a couple of times, and settled down, the last six inches of his tail still wagging.

Canute had a home of his own, now.

John did not sleep well. He had supposed that

everything would run smoothly once they got spaceborne and overcame the problems of escape from Standard. Instead, the purebred group seemed to be fragmenting. Every member was an individual with his own culture and his own interests, and these did not mesh neatly with each other. In the enclaves there had been little real friction, and he realized now that this was because the supporting cast of Standards had been playing parts. In this sense their present group was better, because people had to live real lives and have real interactions before they could get into real arguments. That didn't make those differences pleasant! John felt a cold ripple of anger whenever he thought of Humé's overbearing attitude. It was to this primitive that John would have to turn over the leadership of the group once they landed on earth. That galled him increasingly. How could an African native know anything about twentieth-century or twenty-fourth-century problems? What would become of the purebreds?

Then there was Ala. He liked Ala, for no reason he could pin down, and this made him more conscious of the differences between their cultures. She wore gold earrings that no American girl could afford, yet lived in some mud-brick hovel. John was sure he would not tolerate life in Songhai for more than a few days and that Ala would not appreciate American life, either—apart from the fact that both of their existences were artificial. They would all have to come to terms with

Standard—or with whatever planet earth had become.

The sleeping schedule degenerated, and John didn't try to correct it. One stateroom became the boys' bedroom, anytime; the other, the girls'. Anybody could be up or down at any given moment. The ship moved on.

Then pursuit developed. John had been making a routine check, questioning the ship's communicator about various matters, and learned of this almost by accident.

John alerted the others that they were being followed. "Another spacecraft," he explained, "is traveling a similar course to ours, and gaining. It could be coincidence."

"After we spacejacked this ship? Ha-ha!" Betsy said sourly.

"Change course and see," Humé said. "If it still follows. . . ."

"That would delay our approach to earth," John pointed out. "And if it *is* after us, we would be tipping our hand. Right now it is gaining slowly. It could speed up."

"Do we have any weapons?" Pei asked.

"No," Humé said. "I have been looking. This is a pleasure craft. There is nothing that will strike through space."

"Why don't we just run?" Betsy said. "Maybe we can get to earth before it catches us."

"Not if it is armed," Humé said grimly. "The

deer never escapes the lion, once marked for the kill.''

They looked at John. He was the captain.

Canute passed through the room, heading for his water dish.

"That dog!" Betsy exclaimed. "They're zeroing in on him again!"

"Oh, don't start that," John said, disgusted.

"He's been the cause of trouble all along. A spy in our midst, one way or another. We should put him out the port."

"A fine animal like this?" Humé demanded, surprising John. "He is a member of our group. He is no spy."

"How do you know?" Betsy asked, displeased.

Humé put his hand out, snapping his fingers. "I know animals. Here, Canute!"

The dog came to him, tail wagging. Humé patted the white head.

Ala turned to John. "What is your decision about the ship?"

"Nothing. We'll ignore it and see what happens." John waited for argument, but there was none.

It turned out to be a false alarm. The other ship was not at all close by terrestrial definitions, and in time it deviated from the coincidental course and went its way without ever coming closer than a hundred thousand miles. John's policy had been vindicated, but he felt little relief.

Betsy and Meilan got along worse than ever, and

neither associated with Ala apart from necessary
routine. Pei kept to himself, except for frequent
conversations with Betsy; obviously there was a
rather close relationship forming there that also
irritated Meilan. And Humé. . . .

Humé played with Canute. He defended the dog
against Betsy's complaints and took over both
feeding and cleanup chores. He would strip to a
kind of loincloth and romp with the dog for hours at
a time. Canute would bound over the stress couches
(strewing dog hairs, Betsy said) of the travel
compartment while Humé dived after him. Just as
Humé came close, the dog would dodge aside, and
the friendly chase would begin again. Sometimes
they reversed it, the dog chasing the man.

John hid his jealousy. Once he had played with
Canute like that. Now the dog treated him with a
certain indifference. Sometimes he felt like killing
Humé.

The mood changed one day out from earth. As
the planet appeared on the screen and the ship
began the enormous spiral of the approach, the
tension seemed to lift from each of them, and their
differences became less important. They did not
talk about earth directly but came at it obliquely.

"Are we really so different?" Ala asked. "Do we
have to quarrel about our basic beliefs?"

No! John wanted to cry.

In a moment John, Meilan, and Ala were all

talking at once. Then just as suddenly they stopped, excited and embarrassed.

"We have slightly different physical character-istics," John said, realizing it himself as he spoke. "White, yellow, black—it's only color, a trifling distinction. We're all human beings."

"Can it be," Meilan murmured, "that the Stan-dards are *not* human beings? Why have they separated us from themselves?"

"And from each other," John said. "They tried to stop us from getting together."

"Except for a small mistake. . . ." Ala said.

"*Was* it a mistake?" Meilan inquired. "Or was it merely an intrigue, meant to seem a mistake, to tantalize our curiosity?"

"And was our escape too easy?" John said, picking up the theme. "Did they *want* us to find each other, to make a break for it, fighting off just enough pursuit to convince us that *this* time it was real . . . ?"

"And are they watching and listening now, to learn how well we dance on the string?" Ala continued, "Are we still in the enclave . . . ?"

John looked at the two girls. "I think we'd better call in Pei and Humé and Betsy. We may have some harsh decisions to make."

13

Monument
Earth

"The answer is easy," Humé said. "Destroy the communicator. It is nothing but a spirit ear listening to everything we say. Use the manual controls to land on earth."

"We'd crash," John said immediately. "Without the communicator we'd be a derelict. It is not just an ear; it seems to govern the whole ship."

"We are not entirely helpless," Pei said. "We have tried to run, and perhaps we have only deluded ourselves. Perhaps it is time to negotiate."

"You mean we should offer to stop running if they stop chasing?" John asked. "Just agree to be nice, contented zoo specimens?"

"I doubt we were ever in that category. They could readily have drugged us or put us in real cages. We may be unique but not as exhibits."

"*Ask*," Humé said, irritated by this inaction.

"Communicator—what is our status?"

There was no hesitation. "Monumental," the machine replied.

They had heard it clearly, but what did it mean? That they were very important? That didn't help.

"Please explain," John said nervously.

"It will be better for you to complete your mission. Then you will understand."

"But our mission is to escape to earth!"

"Precisely."

"It balked!" Betsy said, amazed. "I thought it was just an answering service."

John spread his hands, baffled. "I guess they aren't going to stop us. For what that's worth."

"Or *tell* us, either," Betsy added.

"It could be reverse psychology," John said. "Letting us think they *want* us to go to earth so that we *won't* go."

"So let's *go!*" Betsy said.

No one disagreed.

Earth looked just like Standard: cloudy. The ship spiraled down, taking its predetermined time, and they waited with what patience and tension their separate natures provided. As they got down in the atmosphere, the viewscreen became foggy, from either the clouds or some type of interference, and they had to trust to the program entirely. John was perversely gratified: They certainly *would* have crashed on manual.

At last the ship touched down.

"Let's move out," Humé said. It irked John that the African had not waited for any offer or ceremony. He had simply assumed command.

But the port would not phase open. "Don suits," the communicator said.

"Suits? This is earth!" John said.

There was no answer.

"Survey visually," Humé said, and John obeyed, though the order rankled.

The screen now showed a smoky plain, barren of building or tree. "Looks as if there had just been a forest fire," John said, "or a volcanic eruption. All burned out."

"Where *are* we, on earth?" Betsy asked the communicator.

"Monument Washington America, landing zone."

"*Monument* America? As in—well—gravestone? Is it dead?"

"Yes."

She looked at the bleak image again silently. John had some notion of her thoughts, for he shared them. *This* was their heritage?

Humé emerged from the supply room bearing an armful of paraphernalia. He handed a limp outfit to each of them. John donned his suit listlessly. The drive had gone out of him. He was sickly certain that all they would find outside was more devastation. No wonder the Standards weren't worried! Where could the captives go when all that was outside the enclaves, away from Standard, was this?

The suit inflated, sealing itself about him. It was not at all heavy, and it flexed jointlessly as he moved, offering no substantial resistance. The others seemed like mannequins—fat of limb and body, bulbous of head, yet obviously human. Their inflated helmet pieces were opaque on top and translucent around the sides, so as to protect the head from glare; but each face was fully visible.

Canute came up, tail wagging hopefully. He didn't want to be left behind! "Sorry, dogleg," John said. "No suit for you."

Tail down, the dog went to Humé. Humé hesitated, then returned to the storage room. John thought he was going for one of the pseudo-bones as consolation, but he emerged with another suit. It was an animal suit! It was quadrupedal and adjustable, with a bellowslike torso and straps to secure it about feet, tail, and head. It looked as though it could be adapted to fit almost any canine or feline in Canute's approximate weight range. Humé had taken the trouble to check out the ship's supplies carefully and so had been prepared.

Canute was not entirely pleased with the outfit. For one thing it prevented him from scratching himself or nipping at fancied fleas. But he tolerated it as just one more of the strange requirements of human association. He gave a muffled *woof!* inside his egg-shaped helmet and wagged his padded tail.

Only when all suits were tight would the port

phase open. There didn't seem to be any mechanism for interpersonal communications, so they had to shout loudly in their separate enclosures in order to be heard, and then their words were badly muffled.

They filed out. John held his breath as the dust swirled around him, but his air remained pure. Heat ripples showed wherever he looked, but his body was comfortable. This suit, like other Standard equipment, was more sophisticated than it seemed from the outside.

Humé touched his helmet to each of the others in turn and shouted instructions. To John he said: "Rear guard. Watch behind us."

John nodded, still sullen. He would have preferred to argue but knew he was being immature. Humé *was* their leader now, by common agreement, and a rear guard *was* necessary, and somebody *did* have to do it. The others were watching the sides and the ground and the sky while Humé led the way.

Canute tried to sniff the ground, but his helmet frustrated that, so he contented himself with circling the group constantly. Had Humé given the dog instructions, too?

They trekked about half a mile, and the barrens were unchanged. It was getting boring. The communicator had spoken truly: Earth was dead. They could walk until they died and find nothing but desert.

John stared right at it for five or six seconds

before it registered. The back side of one of the rubble-rocks they had passed was flat, and a metal plaque was set in it. Civilization! John started to run toward the marker but remembered his assignment. He had to warn the others in case the thing were booby-trapped!

"Humé!" he yelled, but no one heard. He ran to Meilan, who was watching the left, took her arm, and pointed. She nodded and went to the next in line, gesturing. Then Canute came around on another circuit, herding the people together as though they were sheep. "Fetch Humé!" John yelled, and the dog bounded off.

Soon they were all looking at it from a respectable distance. Humé gestured to the others to wait while he circled the stone. He scooped up a rock and hurled it with impressive force and accuracy so that it bounced off the plaque. When nothing happened, he approached it and studied the writing. Finally he waved the others in.

The plaque was in English—as it should be, for the American sector, John realized. Probably whatever monuments they had in China or Africa were in symbols or Arabic. Only John and Betsy could read this one. It said: *Comfort Station*. That was all.

Betsy's laughter resounded tinnily. She stepped up to the stone and felt along the top with her suited hand. There was a button just above the plaque, and she pressed it.

The ground quivered, then became fluid. John

jumped away as his feet sank in, and the others did the same. "Deadfall!" Humé cried thinly, and Canute yelped.

They had been standing on a shaped, opaque ground panel. Now its pseudo-sand had phased out, and a pit gaped. But it was not a trap. A ramp led downward under the marker, and an archway showed. It was just another Standard device: an entrance to the comfort station.

Humé exchanged glances with the others, then shrugged and led the way down. The panel phased closed above them, and a gentle illumination developed from the floor. At the bottom there was a second curtain that phased open as they approached. Beyond that was a Standard octagonal residential and refreshment chamber.

They removed their helmets, letting their suits deflate. The suits had not been tiring, but the continual buffeting by the blowing dust and the roughness of the terrain had taken their natural toll.

"We never left Standard," Ala said at last.

The others nodded, knowing what she meant. What use was it to travel from one world to another when nothing was changed? They were still unable to operate without drawing on Standard arrangements.

"So do we give up now?" Betsy asked bitterly. "That's what the communicator meant, isn't it? That we'd discover our own futility. . . ."

She trailed off as John gestured toward the speaker vent of the comfort station's apparatus.

They still could not hold a private conversation—if that made any difference now.

"I doubt it," Pei said, answering Betsy's second question. "It classified us as 'monumental,' and that is still not clear. We have not yet found what we came for."

"Does it exist—what we came for?" Meilan asked.

"If this is a typical standard unit. . . ." John began.

"It's *not* typical," Betsy said. "All the cubicles are open at once. No rotation."

She was right. It was probably the only compartment in the area, and outside was nothing but desert.

"Well, you're the leader," John told Humé.

Humé looked nervous. "I am a warrior. This—this is not war as I know it."

Somehow this went far to dispel John's dislike of him. Humé was aware of his own limitations. He knew when to call it quits.

"Communicator," Meilan asked suddenly, "what are we here to learn?"

"You are here to appreciate your temporal and cultural framework."

"In this desert? What *is* our framework?"

"The monument of earth."

"It's still talking riddles!" Betsy exclaimed angrily.

Meilan was unperturbed. "Earth is dead. We are living. How can we be part of this monument?"

"You are sample manifestations of the history and culture of *Homo sapiens*—the animate portion of the monument."

"Thus we are monumental," Pei murmured.

"The history of man," Betsy said, thoughtful now. "His development, his wars, his manners, religions, and races. Through all time. That's an interesting kind of monument."

"Race against time," John said. "That's what we are—three sample races, each set in an appropriate place and time. Very clever contrast of settings."

"How did earth die?" Meilan asked the communicator.

"The monuments illustrate."

Pei smiled. "You need to be more specific in your phrasing. Obviously it isn't going to tell you the entire history of a world in one instant, especially since that seems to be the job the monuments are equipped to do. This is merely the—comfort station."

"How did T'ang die?" she asked, undaunted.

"The monuments illustrate."

"Where can we find the T'ang monument?"

The communicator gave a series of digits—a long series.

"The coordinate of the monument at Wei," Pei said. "That one alone. The real Wei, not the mock-up on Standard."

"Data insufficient."

It was Meilan's turn to smile. "The coordinate of

the monument where the Middle Kingdom city of Wei once stood."

The communicator gave it.

"But this is *earth*!" Betsy protested. "What's it doing with Standard coordinates?"

"Why not?" John asked her. "They can apply their system to one planet as easily as to another. *We* use feet and miles wherever we are."

"How do we reach the Wei monument?" Meilan asked it.

"Summon a conveyance."

"I prefer to learn of Songhai," Ala said.

Humé finally reasserted his leadership. "We shall take turns. We shall return to our ship and travel to each monument in turn. First Wei, then——"

"Mopti," Ala put in.

"And finally——"

"Newton," John said.

"After we have seen our monuments and learned what we can from them, we shall decide what to do," Humé said.

Pei and Meilan went out to see their monument alone. The remaining four stayed in the ship and played tournament tick tack toe. No one had the nerve to conjecture about the report that might emanate from the Middle Kingdom.

Two hours later the two returned. Pei looked shaken, and Meilan had been crying. John reminded himself that the Chinese empires had been ravaged repeatedly by civil wars, changes of dynasty, and foreign conquests, though the essential culture always reasserted itself in a few decades or centuries. To Pei and Meilan that history was the future, real and personal. Had they seen Wei razed by the Mongols? The populace ravaged by the British, the Japanese? Or were worse things buried within that vast history he hardly comprehended? *What had they seen?*

"Mopti," Humé said quietly.

The ship lifted, slanted, dropped. Again the dust and clouds concealed any view they might have had.

Humé and Ala departed. Neither Pei nor Meilan seemed inclined to socialize yet, so John played cryptics with Betsy: Each would invent a simple letter-transposition, apply it to some familiar quotation, and give the coded message to the other to solve. Both were having trouble, because it was hard to concentrate.

Meilan cried silently for a time, and Pei put his arm about her shoulders in the first open display of affection either had shown. Betsy, aware of it, kept her eyes fixed on the code sentence. John could understand her mixed jealousy and compassion. Those two had shared a traumatic experience that brought them together.

John solved his riddle first. "Thucydides!" he cried. " 'To famous men all the earth is a sepulcher.' "

"Yes!" Meilan exclaimed and cried some more.

Both John and Betsy were taken aback. The quotation did have an uncomfortable relevance!

Finally Humé and Ala returned. Humé was angry, his large hands clenching and unclenching, but he was not shattered. Ala looked once at John, lips tight, and turned away.

The slave trade! He knew at once that she had seen it and that anything that might have been between them was over. Why hadn't he realized before that this would happen? He could have warned her. Humé, the warrior, understood the realities of war, conquest, and exploitation; Ala did not. She was a citizen of civilized Songhai.

But now it was the white man's turn. "John, I'm afraid," Betsy whispered, taking his hand in a way she had not done before. He nodded, dry-mouthed, but they had to go.

14

Decision

Newton Monument: just a short trek through the desert. It was an empty, transparent octagon-floored structure fifty feet on a side. John and Betsy entered by phasing directly through the entrance wall and doffed their suits. Outside the perpetual dust storm raged visibly but silently; inside it was pleasant.

"Now what?" Betsy mused, looking about.

"There must be a starting button somewhere."

Near the door panel they discovered a button marked *Inauguration of sequence*. John depressed it.

"Welcome, Stans," the communicator voice said. "This is Monument America, location north-central, number fifteen. This structure commemorates the significant history of the ground covered by this structure."

Betsy looked perplexed. "How's that again?"

"It's the history of a hundred feet square!" John exclaimed, intrigued. "The area, I mean. You know—anything that happened *right here*."

"Oh? What about the rest of America? History doesn't happen just in one place, you know, even when that one place is Newton."

"Guess we'd better play along and find out." But he was dubious himself. As far as he knew, Newton had no significant history—not where world events were concerned. It was strictly backwater. Yet here was the monument.

The voice was silent, and they had nothing to contemplate but a level floor and the brown swirl outside.

"There's a line on the floor," Betsy said. "Almost a path. Do you suppose . . . ?"

As she walked along it, the voice resumed, causing her to stop. "Circa forty-five thousand B.S.E.—Before Standard Era—the first man passed this site. A single *Homo sapiens neanderthalensis*, probably garbed and armed as you see. . . ."

Here a man appeared, startling them. He walked through the wall and into the center of the chamber, glancing occasionally to left and right. He was stocky and hirsute, barely five feet tall, with a flat-vaulted head and pronounced brow ridges and no apparent chin, yet in a hat and a suit he could have mixed with the populace of modern Newton. He wore leather, the fur side in, and carried a wooden spear, a wicked-looking stone hand ax, and an

assortment of flint implements. One of these fell
from his crude belt when his attention was distracted by a flying hawk and remained lost in the
ground cover: the sole evidence of his passage.

"No further visitations occurred at this time,"
the voice said. "Settlement of this hemisphere was
erratic and largely unsuccessful, perhaps because of
limited technology and unfavorable climatic
conditions."

Betsy started to say something as the voice
stopped but decided on action instead. She moved a
little farther along the line, and the commentary
continued.

"Circa fifteen thousand B.S.E. *Homo sapiens*
appeared in force, admitted to the continent by a
temporary contraction of the Laurentide ice sheet
and the Rocky Mountain sheet before the rise in
ocean level blocked the Bering corridor. In this
region mastodons were hunted."

There was a rousing presentation of that portion
of a mastodon chase that occurred on the immediate
site. John was fascinated, never having realized that
elephants once lived wild in America. But Betsy,
impatient to get to more recent events, began
walking slowly along the line. The scene vanished
in mid-hunt, and a new lecture began. But Betsy
did not stop.

John followed, since there was nothing else to do
unless he wanted to make an issue of it. He could
always run the sequence through again later, if it
came to that. So he was treated to tantalizing

glimpses of the various hunting and food-gathering cultures of this region, each fragment some hundreds or thousands of years after the last.

This site was apparently astride the major north-south corridor between the retreating ice sheets, and tribes migrating from Asia through Alaska had to pass here before debouching into the main continent. Thus there was fairly constant turmoil until the ice age passed. Around 10,000 B.S.E. the culture was nomadic, the hunters bringing down seemingly inexhaustible American bison. By circa 7000 the plain grew dry and hot, the large game left, and only the gatherers were able to make a bare living. The climate ameliorated by 4000, bringing the bison back. By 2000 a village of pottery-making, burial-mound-building Amerinds occupied the site, doing some limited farming.

In 1600 B.S.E.—John translated this into his terms as A.D. 500 to 800—more sophisticated agricultural tribes encroached from the east, settling and absorbing the natives. The newcomers were the Siouan. The Caddo moved up from the south, building earth-covered lodges, and their subgroup, the Pawnee, hunted at the site. Finally a migration of quite a different nature developed: The white man came, bringing horses and guns. The French explored and dominated the region; then it passed over to the Spanish, then back to the French. In 292 it was purchased by the recently emerging Union.

"The Louisiana Purchase!" John cried. "That was 1803!"

Betsy ignored him and walked on.

"The Goths were originally from Sweden," the narrator said. "Teutonic barbarians who migrated across the Baltic Sea in the fifth century B.C., displacing the Scythians and Sarmatians there. Then down across the plains of southern Russia toward Hungary and the valley of the Danube, where they settled in the second century A.D. In this period the Goths became excellent horsemen and learned the use of a vital device, the stirrup. With this equipment a heavy cavalryman could keep his seat in the saddle and sustain the shock of the lance's impact."

"This is American history?" Betsy demanded. "They aren't even using B.S.E. dates!"

John watched the scene, confused but fascinated. Mounted, vaguely knightlike horsemen were charging across a plain, their long lances leveled. The narrator explained how, under pressure from the Huns, the Visigoths and Ostrogoths had moved into Roman territory and encountered difficulty there.

". . . Adrianople in 378. Emperor Valens drew up the Roman imperial army in the historic fashion, legions massed in the center, and attacked. . . ."

"It's Roman history!" John cried. "It really *is*!"

"What's it doing *here*?" Betsy said.

But John was already absorbed in the unfolding battle. The Roman infantry was advancing against the Gothic footmen. John was sure the Romans would win, since he knew they had formed one of the most powerful empires of all time. He was mistaken. Goth horsemen appeared at the side, charging against the Roman flank and sweeping the infantry before them. The carnage was appalling, and the Roman army was wiped out.

"Thus medieval warfare was instituted in Europe by the Goths," the narrator said, "and the thousand-year-long dominance of the heavy cavalry in. . . ."

The voice and image vanished. Betsy had stepped forward again.

"In 228 B.S.E. the territory the site occupied was admitted to the Union as the state of Nebraska, but the site itself was unremarkable. It was part of a field of barley situated somewhere between the South Loup and Platte rivers. In 110 the barley diminished and died, the victim of environmental pollution."

Betsy stopped walking.

". . . most serious menace to life on earth," the voice was saying. "It developed first in the most populous and industrial regions but spread rapidly until no portion of earth, sea, or atmosphere was untainted. This site was only marginally affected"—the picture showed a weedy waste— "and the renovation program of 105 brought it back to full yield." Now the field was verdant again.

"Newton!" John said. "Where is Newton? This is the site of Newton, Nebraska. We've passed 1960. . . ."

"Oh, be quiet," Betsy snapped. "That was an enclave on Standard. There was never any such place on earth."

Chastened, he shut up. But it was like the death of a friend.

". . . the solution," the voice continued. "But this was illusory. The problem was international in scope. The advanced nations suffered first and so defined the problem first and acted accordingly, and this eliminated the worst offenders and gave the world a stay of execution. But industrial technology was spreading explosively, and its early phase necessarily brought massive pollution—chemical, radioactive, thermal, sonic, aesthetic. Thus the nations who had reduced their personal standard of living in the interest of a sanitary environment saw their efforts dissipated by the excesses of the emergents, who could not yet afford to apply restraints or limit themselves to nonpollutant sources of power. By 80 B.S.E. the second crisis was at hand. . . ."

The field was a waste again. This time not even the weeds could grow.

"As with most conflicts of national interest, it came swiftly to war. Conventional weapons were banned, however, for they were themselves formidable polluters. This war was muted, undeclared, apolitical—but still savage. The killing stroke was bacterial—a plague strain against which the populaces of the favored nations were inoculated in advance."

The scene showed a man staggering through the barren field. His face was swollen and greenish, his eyes so bloodshot as to have no whites. He clutched at his throat as though he could not breathe and fell, to gasp a few times before shuddering to stillness.

"The inoculant did not reach every citizen of the favored," the narrator observed, "nor was it denied every citizen of the unfavored." There was no picture for that, of course, since only local scenes were shown.

"Ninety percent of the outcast peoples died in the first strike, and twenty percent of the poor, the old, and the racial, ethnic, or religious minorities in the favored nations."

Betsy turned to John, white-faced. "They played politics—with genocide!" she whispered, appalled.

John felt cold. "They'll pay—*we'll* pay," he said. "We *have* paid—that's why this country is a desert now."

"The few survivors of that bacterial strike in the unfavored regions turned ferociously against the favored and succeeded in destroying the secret factories and laboratories that manufactured the inoculant. Both plague-strain and inoculant were artificial. The human body tended to manufacture antibodies against both. This hardly slowed the plague, because it was usually fatal within sixty hours of infection; but it nullified the inoculant in the system in the course of months. Every three months a revised formula had to be administered to counteract this. Thus with the loss of the laboratories the favored were doomed to the same extinction as the unfavored."

"Enough!" Betsy cried, stepping forward to cut off the sight of well-dressed white men and women and children staggering through the field, gasping and falling. Again there were only glimpses and snatches of lecture: world population falling from billions to millions, "pures" of any color systematically hunted and butchered, the entire world laid waste. The field became figuratively buried in bones. By the time the survivors had renovated a factory and produced a trickle of new inoculant, the plague had spent itself. Perhaps one percent of the population of the world had turned out to be naturally immune.

In the virtual absence of man, however, the environment slowly recovered. The land turned green again. Flowers appeared between the skeletons of the Newton site.

Man survived in the form of the Standards. Naturally resistant to the plague and of indeterminate race, they shaped their culture around an intense aversion to waste or pollution in any form. They had few animals and fewer other resources, but the complete technology of mankind was available. In a century they had recovered the level of affluence enjoyed by their predecessors, though only a fraction of the numbers. This was the first century S.E., Standard Era.

By the end of the second century S.E. they had surpassed the previous pinnacle of civilization handily. Their numbers remained deliberately low, and conservation and renovation remained their effective religion, but their society became stagnant. This did not disturb the majority, for that was the definition of the malady: that the majority sought no change. But an activist minority feared for the future and conjectured that the same rigid uniformity that promoted peace and plenty and an amicable environment was stifling the creativity and drive of the species.

There were, it developed, procreative banks dating from the period when many races existed on earth. It was possible to nurture infants of those races who would, genetically, be as "pure" as any races had ever been, though their societies were long extinct. Here on the Newton site an imaginary town was built, incorporating all the known elements of one of those societies. John's town of Newton appeared in the image.

John and Betsy, shocked, did not need to listen to the rest. They now understood their place in this scheme. Parentless and rootless, they were called monuments, to justify the project and nullify the formidable Standard prejudice against their deviant type. They were called living monuments, but they were more than that. Much more.

"Now we know," Pei said. "There may have been mistakes in the program, and perhaps they underestimated us, but we remain very much in the Standard world."

"*Mistakes!*" Humé said. "That blunder when Meilan was sent to visit me—total incompetence."

"Not to mention things like letting Roman history leak into American history—and never correcting it," John said.

"To a flea, the lion seems stupid," Ala murmured. "Yet the flea needs the lion more than the lion needs the flea."

"They underestimated us because their culture is in stasis," Betsy said. "A planetary bureaucracy that can't even keep track of its ID cards or organize an effective pursuit!"

"Perhaps they are merely more civilized than we," Meilan said. "They would hesitate to use such violent methods and would not know how to react to violence. So they delayed while we continued."

"So maybe we *are* different," John said. "Those procreative banks—they wouldn't have represented the dull or unfit, exactly. High I.Q. stock. Maybe we *will* accomplish more—given the chance."

"We shall *take* the chance!" Humé said.

"But there is nothing left for us on earth!" Ala protested. "We have nowhere to go but Standard."

"Surely you realize that Standard *is* earth," Pei said.

John choked back his exclamation, hiding his ignorance.

Meilan nodded agreement. "Remember those alternate coordinates? We wondered how the system could work, when each coordinate identified *two* places on the globe. Now we know that one is always for Standard, the other for earth. The

Standards renovated their own half but left the rest as a perpetual monument to the mistakes of the past. So that man would never forget."

John was dismayed. "So we never really left the planet! We just spiraled around for two weeks! I never thought to check the proximity of Standard once we were on our way."

"It was a necessary period," Pei said kindly. "We had to have time to get to know each other."

"Necessary!" Betsy said indignantly. "It was a dirty trick!"

John liked her better for that.

"Necessary," Pei repeated firmly. "We *are* of different cultures, and they do not mix readily except when under common stress. The conventions of dress, diet, religion. . . ."

John remembered. Yes, they were different—and he was not about to refute his basic beliefs for the sake of group unity. Betsy was difficult, but she shared his views in the important matters. But what common ground could they have—except that of Standard culture? The language might be the same, but so much else was dismayingly different!

"We *can* work together," Pei said. "For the sake of our freedom, we can compromise—among ourselves, not the Standards. We have done it so far."

"If we become a group of our own, isolated," Ala said slowly, "and married between the races, and our children did the same—would not our lineage become Standard?"

That needed no answer. The Standards were the

result of the mixing of the races of mankind. The moment the purebreds crossed the racial lines, their distinction vanished.

"I think," Meilan said quietly, "that the enclaves are a worthy project, after all."

And there it was. What could they accomplish as refugees that would improve on what the activist Standards had in mind? The world of the Standards was the real world now, and that was where the changes had to be made. If race were the answer to species vitality, it would be a crime to destroy what had been done so far, but it rankled John mightily. He had fought hard for his independence; was he now meekly to acquiesce, admitting that all his aspirations had been wrong?

"But that leaves us even more isolated—from the Standards and from each other," Betsy said. "Whom will our children marry?"

"There are other cells in the procreative banks," the ship's communicator said, startling them. "If the pilot group succeeds, many more purebreds will be raised, replacing the Standards presently in the enclaves."

It would succeed if only they let it, John realized. Gradually the enclaves would become genuine, as more and more true Caucasians, Negroids, and Mongoloids filled them. Why, then, did he still have this urge to fight?

"But we don't have to live in ignorance!" he cried. "We can visit each other, we can study the Standard technology without being corrupted by

it—" He broke off, realizing that his words sounded very much like agreement instead of dissent. His
spirit was more aggressive than his voice! Yet a part
of him was looking forward to seeing Mom and
Dad again, going on to college. . . .

He could tell by their silence that the others were
accepting it also. Let them all go back—for a while.
Soon they would be grown, more knowledgeable,
better able to cope with the world of the Standards.

His eye caught Humé's. Slowly the African
winked. John did not need to look at Pei and Meilan
to know that the empire of T'ang agreed. Guerrilla
tactics: Bide your time until the moment was right.
Then strike.

The Standards did not need race; they needed an
example. The world did not need monuments; it
needed action. All history was witness to that! John
smiled. The Standards didn't know it, but they had
wrought well. There would be a world of action—at
the proper time.

Canute came up to him, tail wagging halfhearted-
ly. John looked over the dog's head to see Humé
watching. "I think you'll be happier in Kanem,
coach dog," John said sadly. "I have no right to
hold you. Go with Humé." He blinked to keep the
tears from forming. There was a society to save; he
couldn't weaken now! "But come visit me. . . ."
He could not continue.

"He will," Ala said. "Often. I will see to it."

Now Betsy was smiling, too.

TURN THE PAGE FOR THE NEXT EXCITING BOOK BY PIERS ANTHONY

HASAN

COMING FROM TOR BOOKS IN JANUARY

"Gold!—from copper?" Hasan's loose headcloth fluttered with his impolite laughter.

The white-bearded Persian nodded gravely. He was dressed in a handsome robe and wore sturdy sandals: a man of moderate wealth. He looked remarkably pious under his tall white turban—but Persians were in bad repute in Bassorah.

Hasan had seen the man move slowly down the street, investigating the crowded stalls on either side. This was the metalworkers' section of the city, and there were splendid displays of copper, silver and gold, all intricately wrought. Many were far more spectacular than Hasan's own—yet the Persian had paused longest here, exclaiming to himself and shaking his head.

Hasan soon concluded there was little prospect for a sale, for otherwise the customer would have demeaned the merchandise in an effort to reduce its

price. He pretended to read an old book, fretfully
waiting for the intruder to move on and leave the space
clear for some legitimate client.

Why did he linger so? Could he be a bandit from the
marshes to the north, hiding from the Caliph's justice
amidst the towering reeds? Impossible; yet—

At the hour of the mid-afternoon prayer the shops
cleared of customers, but the Persian remained. Hasan
did not trust him. All True Believers went to prayer-
call promptly. There was something furtive in the way
the man's eyes shifted about, though his voice was
cultured and persuasive enough.

"Young man, you are a most talented craftsman.
Your father trained you well."

"I have no father," Hasan replied shortly, trying to
maintain his prejudice in the face of such flattery.

The Persian became unctuous. "Ah, the good man
has joined Allah—may His name be praised. And I—I
have no son." Hasan grew uncomfortable under the
man's intense scrutiny. "Yet I could hardly ask for a
finer son than you. Your locks are as long and black as
the mane of a fine stallion. Your body is straight and
strong. If I had a son like you, I would weigh him
down with wealth beyond tabulation."

"Wealth?" Hasan said, too quickly.

"Provided he didn't object to a little innocent
alchemy, in a good cause."

"Alchemy!" This was forbidden in Bassorah.

"How else is an honest merchant to convert
common copper, or even brass, into an equal weight—
of gold?" The Persian's eye was fixed upon Hasan's,
challenging him to protest.

And Hasan had laughed—but not for long. "If you

can do such a thing—change copper to gold—why are you shopping here? You could be rich in a single day."

The Persian shook his head in seeming sadness. "And what are riches, to one who has no son?" An artful tear coursed down one wrinkled cheek, "I have no wife, no concubine, for how am I to trust a woman, and I an alchemist? Many man have begged me to instruct them in my secret art, and I have refused them all. But love of you has gotten hold upon my heart, for you are the fairest lad in all the city, and if you will consent to become my adopted son I will teach you this skill. You will toil no more with hammer and anvil; you will sweat no more in the heat of the charcoal and fire. No, not one more day!"

The old man was beginning to make sense. "Teach me now," Hasan said, maintaining his guard, for he suspected a swindle in spite of his desire to be convinced.

"Tomorrow," the Persian said. "I will bring my preparations here early in the morning, and you must make ready some copper. I do not ask you to believe until you see this for yourself, my son." With that he departed, leaving Hasan both doubtful and wildly excited.

Gold! Could it be?

He was too disturbed to finish the day patiently in his stall. He closed up shop and tramped blindly out of the city, his head spinning. Gold! Key to rich living. He would dine on candied locusts and choice Persian stew. He would sip sweet sherbert from the colored glass of Sidon. He would garb himself in a robe of embroidered damask, and sleep under a sheet of finest oriental silk. Choice slave-girls would fan away the biting flies while he dispensed largesse to groveling beggars and needy holy men and thus store up great favor with Allah.

He looked up to see the dry mud flats, cut by shallow irrigation ditches, that stretched from the two great rivers toward the foul marshes. The People of the Reeds dwelt in floating huts, not so far away, neighbors of unclean pigs. They sat with their vicious dogs around fires of buffalo dung. Hasan knew little of them for civilized men were not welcome in the reedy swamps. There had been occasional skirmishes . . .

He turned back to face the city. Gold! The cultivated fields became rosy in the glow of dusk, the hot sands saffron. Clustered date-palms beckoned in a momentary gust of wind, and swarms of sea-fowl dotted the sky, calling him to his destiny.

The sun sank, and Hasan quickly spread out his prayer-mat, and kneeled with his face to the distant west of Mekkeh. He prostrated himself ritually and called upon Allah for blessing. Gold!

His old, careworn mother was cynical. Hasan sat barefooted on a cushion of the divan, leaned against the plastered wall, and smacked his lips on stale bread and sour camel's milk while she harangued him about the business of the day. She was adept at prying and wheedling information that didn't concern her, he thought, as were all women whom time had deprived of physical charm. She had the story from him almost as he entered the run-down dwelling.

"Hasan, don't pay attention to such superstitions. Beware especially of Persians, and never do anything they urge upon you. They are nothing but infidels and sharpers, and if this man pretends to alchemy you can be sure it is only to steal the money of an honest man."

"But we are poor, Mother," Hasan pointed out rudely, half lost in his dreams of wealth. The good house, now suffering from lack of repair, was all that remained of their original fortune. "How could he covet the little bit of gold I have in the shop, when he has the power to manufacture as much as he wants, from copper?"

She looked at him despairingly. "How can you trust the word of a stranger—a Persian!—who makes such a ridiculous promise? Have you forgotten already the leeches and loafers who promised you their undying friendship—until the wealth your father left was exhausted catering to their expensive tastes? And where are these friends now? Where would *you* be now, were it not for the kindness of your father's friend, the goldsmith, who took you in and taught you his trade?"

"But I am tired of this trade," Hasan said defensively. "I thought all goldsmiths were rich, but—"

"But, but!" she exclaimed. "My son, Bassorah is a wealthy city, for this is where the long sea meets the richest farmland east of Egypt. The traders come here in great number, and the boatsmen and camel-drivers and farmers. But you can't expect to make your fortune as a goldsmith without working for it. All day you sit idly in your shop and read books about the adventures of liars like that Sindbad of the Sea, instead of calling out to passing merchants who might pay you well for your effort. No wonder you sell nothing!"

"I'm sure this Persian is honest," Hasan argued uncertainly. "He wears a turban of pure white muslin, in the best manner of the True Believer. And he wants to adopt me as his son!"

He ignored her look of reproach and retired, but sleep was slow in coming. Gold!

Hasan woke at dawn, performed the morning ablution, and rushed to his shop without speaking to his mother. Anxiously he cast about for copper; this was a detail he'd almost forgotten. It would not be wise to use a finished utensil, because if anything were to go wrong the loss would be awkward, particularly when his mother learned of it. Ah—there was a broken platter that would have to be melted down anyway. It was copper, or at least good brass, and it should do well enough.

Before long the Persian appeared. Hasan jumped up. "Welcome, Oh noble Uncle! Let me kiss your venerable hands!"

The Persian restrained him. "We must do this business quickly, before the neighboring smiths arrive, or everyone will know the secret. Have you heated the furnace?"

"Oh yes, Uncle!"

"Set up the crucible and apply your bellows."

Hasan hastened to comply, forgetting in his eagerness yesterday's promise of freedom from such labors. The fire blazed up hotly, until it seemed the crucible itself would melt.

"Where is your copper?"

"Here, Uncle!"

"Take your shears and cut it into small pieces and melt them down promptly."

Hasan was amazed at the businesslike air of the man who yesterday had waxed so sentimental. He followed the terse instructions, sweating profusely under his tunic from the unaccustomed heat and effort. The metal became a thick liquid as he wrestled mightily with the bellows.

The Persian inspected it approvingly. He removed his turban, reached inside, and brought out a folded wad of paper. A few ounces of yellow powder were inside. "Stand back, boy," he said, "but don't let up for a moment on the bellows."

Hasan pumped until he thought he would expire, while still trying valiantly to observe every detail of the magic.

The old man held the paper above the crucible. "In the name of Jabir ibn-Hayyan, the father of alchemy, and by virtue of this catalyst he created and bequeathed to me in dire secrecy, let this base metal be converted forthwith to purest gold!" He shook in some of the bright powder.

It seemed to Hasan that the pot bubbled angrily and that an ominous glow suffused the room. This was evil magic, and the Persian had not invoked the name of Allah. . . .

"Hold!" and Hasan relaxed gratefully. He wiped his smarting eyes and peeked into the crucible.

Gold.

"Test it," said the Persian, smiling. "You will find it to be of rare quality."

Hasan quenched it and manhandled the still hot mass out of the pot and rubbed it with a file. It was genuine. He leaned against the counter for support, dazed by the reality. Gold! The magician had not been lying.

The Persian gave him no rest. "Quickly, son, hammer it into an ingot before the merchants come."

Hasan bent hastily to the task, while the Persian watched with an inscrutable expression. "Are you married?"

"No, sir!" The ingot was almost shaped.

"Very good," the old man said to himself, with another appraising glance at Hasan. "Now carry this gold to the market and sell it quickly. Don't waste time haggling over the price; as soon as you have a good offer, take the money, go home without a word to anyone, and put it away where no one will see it. We don't want the people to interrogate you about the origin of this gold."

Hasan agreed, although he regretted being denied an immediate spending spree. His mother would insist that he put most of the money back into the goldsmith business, and he would get little pleasure from it. Of course, if she saw the ingot, she might not let him sell it at all, since many fine utensils could be fashioned from it.

He picked up the ingot, which weighed several pounds, wrapped it in a fold of his tunic, and rushed to the richest business section of Bassorah.

The assembled businessmen were amazed at the size and quality of the ingot. Bidding was rapid. "A thousand dinars," a fat purple-cloaked moneychanger offered. Hasan turned his back disdainfully. "Twelve hundred," another said, barely concealing his eagerness to possess such refined gold. Hasan yawned. "Fifteen hundred," a green-pantalooned merchant said.

Hasan studied the last bidder calmly. "Allah open on you another door," he said, in a time-honored convention that indicated too low a bid. That is, Allah would have to open the door to merchandise at such a price, for Hasan certainly wouldn't.

The first moneychanger squinted, catching on to the fact that this young man was not entirely innocent about the value of his merchandise. "Eighteen hundred dinars—no more," he said.

"Allah open—" Hasan said, then remembered the Persian's warning. "This fine gift is a gift at such a price—but I am weary of carrying it. Take it for two thousand dinars."

In such manner he completed the richest transaction of his life.

"Look at this, Mother!" he cried as he burst into the house with the hefty purse of coin. "My father the Persian has shown me how to make gold from a broken platter, and I sold it for half a year's income, and I'm going to be rich!"

The old woman shook her head lugubriously, despite the proof displayed before her, Hasan had forgotten his resolve to hide the news from her. "No good will come of this. It is devil's money." And she blessed herself, saying "There is no majesty and there is no might, except in Allah, the Glorious, the Great!"

"I must take more metal to the shop," Hasan said, paying no attention to her words. He picked up a large metal mortar, a pot once used for crushing onions, garlic and corn cakes. Heedless of his mother's expostulations, he carried it out the door.

The Persian was still sitting in the shop, relaxing in its shade with his turban in his lap. His hair was almost as white as the headpiece. "What are you doing with that thing?" he demanded.

"I'm going to put it on the fire and turn it into gold," Hasan said.

"Have the jinn taken your wits?" the Persian exclaimed, choking. "The surest way to arouse suspicion would be to appear in the market twice a day with mysterious ingots of perfect gold. The merchants would be certain you had stolen them, and this would cost us both our lives."

Hasan was chagrined. "I hadn't thought of that."

"If I am to teach you this craft—and there is more to it than mere sprinkling of powder—you will have to promise to practice it no more than once a year. That will easily bring enough income to maintain you."

"I agree, O my lord!" Hasan said, anxious to master the process. So long as no limit was set upon the amount converted in that annual session. . . .

He placed the crucible over the furnace and heaped more charcoal on the fire.

"Now what are you up to?"

"How am I to learn this craft if we don't go through the steps again?"

"There is no majesty and no might save in Allah!" exclaimed the Persian, laughing at the youth's audacity. "You have the singlemindedness of a thirsty camel, lad. But you hardly demonstrate the wit required for this noble craft. Do you expect to learn such an art in the middle of the street? With all the grasping shoppers and beggars looking on? Don't you know what they do to proven alchemists?"

"But—"

"If you really want to master this mystery immediately, come to my house, where there will be privacy."

"Let's go!" Hasan replied immediately, closing up his shop.

But as he followed the Persian, he began to reflect upon his mother's warning. Such men did have a bad reputation. How could he be certain this was not some elaborate trick to lure him into slavery, perhaps in the uncharted marshland? Handsome young artisans were valuable, and few questions were asked if their tongues were cut out. Did he really know this stranger well enough to trust himself to his house? His feet dragged, and finally he stopped in confusion.

The Persian turned to see him lagging. "Are you having foolish second thoughts *now*, my son? Here I am, trying to do you the greatest favor of the age because of the love I have in my heart for you—while you hang back, accusing me of bad intent!"

Hasan felt quite guilty, but his doubt remained. The man was leading the way out of the city, and it was hard not to suspect pork in the cookpot.

"Ah, the folly of youth!" the Persian expostulated. "Well, boy, if you're afraid to come to my house, I must go to yours. I can teach you there just as easily, so long as you provide the materials."

Hasan brightened. "You can?"

"Show me the way, son."

Hasan's mother was not delighted. "You brought the idolator *here*? I will not share the roof with him!"

"But this way he is proving his good faith. What harm could he do at my house?"

"What harm could a cobra do in your house? A sword-tusked boar? You—"

"He's standing outside our door right now."

"No! He is nothing but a ghoul, an evil influence. I will not remain while he sets foot in this house!"

"But he is teaching me to make gold out of—"

"He is making mush out of your brains. I'll stay at my cousin's house until he is gone." She was already busy setting the house in order, however, lest the unwelcome guest find anything to criticize. At length she finished her preparations and left by the back way, so as not even to see the Persian, and Hasan was free to invite the guest inside. Then he had to run to the market to buy food, while the Persian waited some more.

Hasan spread his best circular cloth on the floor, in the corner near the two divans, and arranged the meal. He set up a stool supporting a large brass tray, upon which were several copper dishes. Around these were round, flat cakes of bread, some cut limes, and small wooden spoons. He had hired a servant-boy for the meal, who now brought large napkins and a basin and ewer filled with water to each of them. They rinsed their mouths and washed their right hands ceremoniously as they sat cross-legged on the two divans. It would never do to eat with an unclean hand.

"In the name of Allah, the Compassionate, the Merciful," Hasan said, serving himself first in accordance with the ritual. This showed that the food he offered his guest was wholesome. He drew a dish of mutton toward him, stewed with assorted vegetables and with apricots, and removed a morsel with the aid of a piece of bread.

The Persian did likewise. For a moment it looked as though he was about to touch the food with his left hand, and Hasan marveled at this. All True Believers knew that the left hand was unclean. It was unthinkable that the hand that cleaned the privates should ever touch the face . . . yet the visitor had almost—

He was imagining things. Even in Persia, they were not that slovenly. He should abolish such unnatural suspicions.

Hasan drank some cool water from a porous earthen bottle. "Praise be to Allah," he said—but did not mention that it had been many weeks since Allah had blessed him with a repast like this.

"May your drink produce pleasure," the Persian replied, also following the ritual. But his gaze was calculating.

"Now there is the fellowship of bread and salt between us," Hasan exclaimed as they ate. "What loyal servant of Allah would violate that?"

"What, indeed," the guest replied dryly.

They finished the meal, and the Persian leaned back, belched politely, but did not wash his hand again. "What did you bring for dessert?"

Hasan stammered in confusion. He had forgotten this detail.

"No trouble, my son. You just run down to the market again and fetch us something suitable, some sweetmeats." He closed his eyes comfortably, anticipating no refusal.

Hasan rose hastily and dashed off, forgetting to send the servant, and returned shortly with an armful of pastries. The Persian eyed the monstrous amount the young man had brought home in his enthusiasm and shook his head with mock perplexity. "O my son—the likes of you delight the likes of me. Nowhere, in all Bassorah, could I have found a *more* appropriate subject for my purposes!" He hardly bothered to conceal the sneer, but Hasan in his naivete flushed with pleasure.

After they had eaten their fill and washed hands and face again, the Persian stretched lazily and uttered the magic words. "O Hasan, fetch the gear."

Hasan shot out of the house like a colt let out to fresh green pasture in the spring. He ran to his shop and carried all the apparatus he could sustain back to the house, once more panting and sweating with the exertion he hoped to be relieved of so soon.

The Persian withdrew from his turban a package of some weight. "My son, this wrapping contains three pounds of the elixir I demonstrated this morning, and each ounce of it will transform a pound of copper into the finest gold. When this is gone, I will make up another batch for you."

Hasan trembled as he took the package and stared at the glittering yellow powder. "What do you call this?" he inquired. "How is it made?"

The Persian laughed far more than the innocent questions deserved.

"Must you know everything at once, boy? There will be time for that later. The manufacture of this elixir is quite complicated; for now you should be satisfied to keep quiet and master its proper application." Hasan did not notice the increasingly overbearing tone or the poor breeding the laughter betrayed. Gold dazzled his mind's eye. He found a brass platter and cut it up and threw the pieces into the melting pot. He blew up the fire until the metal melted, then shook in a little powder and stirred the mixture vigorously. He was so intent on what he was doing that he never thought to call upon Allah for blessing.

Nevertheless, the molten potful steamed up, shimmered, and took on the golden hue. "It worked!" Hasan shouted. "I did it! I made gold!"

He removed his crucible from the heat and fumbled with the tongs as the golden lump cooled. He did not see the Persian break open one of the surplus pastries, shake in a little powder of different complexion and seal it up again. He did not overhear the exuberant chuckle.

"You have done very well, my son," the Persian said. "You seem to have a natural talent for what I have in mind, and I am most pleased with your performance. Did I mention that I have a daughter, who is as lovely a girl as anyone has ever seen?"

Hasan pulled his eye momentarily away from the glistening mass of gold. "Sir, I thought you were unmarried. How can you have a daughter?"

The Persian paused, but corrected himself quickly. "You are astute, my boy. True, I have no wife *now*. I had one, a very discerning and gracious and obedient woman of singular beauty, but she died five years ago and I have brought my daughter up and educated her myself. Since you are to be my adopted son, it seems appropriate that I marry her to you."

Things began to fall into place for Hasan. A marriagable daughter; an offer of unlimited gold. The full commitment was coming to light.

"Well, I hadn't planned to—"

"I assure you, she is no less beautiful than yourself, a fitting match. Her face is like the full moon, her hair darker than the night, her cheeks rosy as—"

"Shouldn't I see her first?" Hasan asked cautiously, disturbed by the manner the Persian seemed to be reading his face.

"Her posture is like a slim bamboo among plants; her eyes are as large and dark as those of a delicate young deer."

"Yes, but—"

"Her two breasts are like fresh round pomegranates; her buttocks are like wind-smoothed hillocks of sand . . . and she is just fourteen years of age!"

"Done!" cried Hasan, carried away by this vision. After all, there was always the gold, in case the damsel fell short of the description.

"Congratulations! Let's celebrate with another

sweetmeat," the Persian said, pressing the one he held on Hasan.

The young man bit into it automatically, careless of all ceremony, thinking of gold and hillocks of sand. Once more he forgot to praise Allah before taking food.

A vacant expression came over his face. He reeled and collapsed, unconscious.

"O dog of an Arab!" the Persian exalted. "O carrion of the gallows! How many months have I searched for as handsome an innocent as you. Yet how near you came to slipping my net. But now I have you! If an elephant smelled that bhang I fed you, he would sleep from year to year."

Nevertheless, he took the precaution of binding Hasan hand and foot, gagging him, and packing him into a great chest, which he locked. Then he gathered together all the money from the sale of the first ingot of gold, and everything else of value in the house including the second ingot, and packed it all into another chest. Before long he had summoned a porter from the market and assigned him the second trunk, instructing him not to drop it. He dallied only long enough to scribble a message on the wall, and departed in haste.

A rented ship, provisioned and crewed, was waiting for him in a special harbor outside the city, in the direction he had attempted to lead Hasan earlier. He paid off the porter, loaded the merchandise on board, and set sail immediately with a fair wind.

What a welcome awaited Hasan's mother when she came home that evening! The door was open, the rooms ransacked, and her cherished son was gone. All that remained were cryptic words printed crudely on one wall, near a half-eaten bit of sweetbread.

The spirit came and wakened one from bed;
But when he woke, he found the spirit fled!

Vinegar and acrid powder choked Hasan, and he came to his senses coughing and sneezing violently. The world seemed to be swaying and tilting in crazy combinations, now one way and now another, so that he could hardly orient himself. He felt sick.

A black ifrit stood before him. "So the Arab pig opens his eyes!" a harsh voice said near his ear. Hasan recognized the voice of the Persian, despite the change in tone. Was he a demon?

His eyes cleared slowly, and he saw that what he faced was not an infernal creature, but a grinning Negro slave, a eunuch. Beyond the slave was a short wooden deck, and beyond that—

He was aboard a ship! He could see the lapping waves, the distant shoreline. No wonder he had reeled to the steady rocking of the floor. He was sitting on one of the great chests his mother had saved, and beside him sat the Persian. How had such a thing come about?

"There is no majesty and there is no might, except in Allah, the Glorious, the Great!" he swore. "We belong to Allah, and to Him we shall return."

"Don't prate your ridiculous faith aboard this ship!" the Persian snapped. "You are in my power now, you incredible simpleton."

Hasan began to understand. He had eaten a pastry this man had handed him—and suddenly found him-

self among strangers and far from home. He had been
drugged! But why?

"Oh my father," he said quietly, "what have you
done? Didn't we eat bread and salt together, so that
neither could betray the other?"

The Persian stared at him. "Do you expect me to be
bound by your superstitions? Your life means nothing
to me, and your friendship less. I have slain nine
hundred and ninety-nine whelps like you, and you
shall surely be the thousandth." His expression was so
serious that Hasan could not doubt that he meant what
he said. All of it had been a trick after all, to lure him
into this situation. His mother's warning had been
valid, and his own early suspicions justified.

He shifted his hands and found them tied behind
him. His feet were free, but he was helpless. Yet
obviously they weren't going to kill him right away;
the ship must have a destination, and a far one, or it
would not have been employed at all. Was he to be a
sacrifice? He had heard of such things, at least in the
far reaches of the world where the jinn-folk lived. He
should be safe for a few days, at least.

Hasan was frightened, but not nearly as much as he
thought he ought to be. Perhaps the drug the Persian
had given him still affected his senses. Still, he had
always longed for adventure and never had the means
to undertake it. Now it had come upon him unawares,
and though the shaft of fate was painful, it was not
wholly repulsive. The Persian might be bluffing,
testing him, trying out his mettle; if not there were a
thousand things that might happen before the sentence
was carried out. Well, perhaps a hundred, or at least
ten. . . .

"Who are you?" he asked the Persian. "What do you want with me?"

The man studied him as if annoyed that there had been no screaming or begging. "I am Bahram the Guebre, the foremost magician of Persia. I will use you to obtain the essential ingredient for my elixir of gold, and you will not survive that use."

"Why don't you kill me now, Bahram?" Hasan was astonished at his own temerity; he had never imagined that he could contemplate death so calmly.

"Don't be impatient, lad; you have three months to live yet; maybe more. I would have killed you before now, if more important considerations didn't restrain this pleasure."

"Do you expect me to live three months without eating?" Hasan asked him. "How good a magician are you?"

The Persian refused to take offense at the tone. "Untie his hands and give him some water," he directed his slave.

The eunuch came forward cheerfully. He was big and wore bright red pantaloons; evidently he had once been muscular, but now was running to fat. His eyes were sleepy, but his hands, as he reached around Hasan to undo the cord, were clever and gentle. "Now tread lightly, Arab," he murmured into Hasan's ear as he worked.

Hasan stretched his arms. His wrists were chafed and stiff where the rope had bound them, but were after all serviceable. He accepted the jug the slave offered. As he drank, his eyes ran over the ship.

It appeared to be a fair-sized merchant ship, built for the open sea. There were no oars—if merchanters carried oarsmen, there would be little space for

cargo—and he could see the tall center mast reaching
up into the single square sail. She might be as much as
forty-five feet from stem to stern—but old. Even
though he was no Sindbad, he could sense the wallow
and see the age of the calking in the worn deck. This
tub would not be worth much in a storm.

Hasan finished his drink and returned the bottle to
the eunuch. "Praise be to Allah," he said, and
launched himself from the chest.

And sprawled on the deck. The slave had neatly
tripped him. He was neither as sleepy nor as stupid as
he looked, that eunuch.

"Tie the ingrate up again," Bahram said. "We
won't give him another chance to betray our trust."

"Betray your trust!" Hasan exploded. "Why you
dog, dog-fathered, grandson of a dog! How can you
act other than as a dog? *Trust!*"

Bahram stood up. "By the virtue of the Heat and
the Light of the Fire I worship, do not tempt me to
violence, boy!"

"What temptation remains for the uncircumcised
cur who foully betrays bread and salt?"

"Silence!" the Persian roared. His hand swung
round to deal Hasan a blow that sent him crashing to
the deck. This time, with his hands bound, he struck
face down. He felt his teeth digging into the dirty
planking as he passed out.

His trial was not over. Sea water dashed in his face
brought him spluttering to his senses a second time.
He knew that only a moment had passed. His nose
stung fearfully in the salt and he could taste the blood
running over his bruised lips. His front teeth felt as
though they had been driven back into his head; angry
tears trickled down his cheeks.

The eunuch propped him up and mopped away some of the mess. "You have more to lose than a few drops of blood, Arab," he murmured, his voice so soft that Hasan knew the magician was not intended to overhear. "Appease his fancies, it won't hurt Allah, the All-knowing."

Hasan nodded, not certain whether this was a genuine condolence or another trap. Certainly he would not again insult the Persian to his face. Not while he was bound, anyway.

"Make a Fire!" Bahram said, and two young boys, white servants, appeared with a brazier. They filled it with charcoal and tinder and struck sparks into it, and soon a hot flame crept up through the chunks. Hasan wondered what would happen if such a stove were to be overturned on the deck. No—the wood had just been soaked down, and would not ignite.

"What is the purpose of that?" Hasan inquired, discovering that his fall had not affected his power of speech, despite the discomfort of teeth and nose.

"This is the Fire, my Lady of Light and Sparkles! She is the goddess I worship, not your foul bread and salt Allah. See how bright She is! How fair!" Indeed, as the magician looked into the flame his expression was rapt, and he stood tall and bold.

Hasan was disgusted, but he held his peace. How could he ever have been fooled by such a creature?

Bahram turned to him, his eyes burning fanatically. "O Hasan—this is my Beloved! Worship Her as I do, and I swear to you I will give you half my wealth and marry you to my maiden daughter. Worship the Fire, and I will set you free and find some other sacrifice." He waited expectantly.

Hasan forgot his recent resolution.

"Woe to you!" he cried out angrily. "You are a criminal who prays to a vanishing element instead of to the True God, the King of the Omnipotent, the Creator of Night and Day. How can you desert the God of the Prophets Moses, Jesus, and the great Mohammed? This is not worship you practice—it is nothing but calamity!"

Bahram stiffened. "O dog of the Arabs, are you refusing to worship with me?"

"I will never turn my face away from Allah!"

The man's eyes smoldered like the coals of the brazier, but he did not strike Hasan again. He faced the fire, dropped to his knees, and prostrated himself before it ritually. "O Sacred Fire, I will punish this infidel for his blasphemy!"

He stood up and spoke to the eunuch. "Cast him on the deck on his face!" The slave obeyed, muttering dolefully into Hasan's ear.

"I told you. I told, Arab. You didn't have to renounce Allah in your heart. 'Appease his fancies,' I said, 'It won't hurt your god,' I said. But you—" Then Hasan hit the deck, more gently this time, and the remaining advice was lost.

"Strip him down," Bahram directed. Hasan felt the eunuch's careful black hands pulling away his tunic, leaving him bare from neck to calf.

"I don't like this any better than you do," the slave muttered as he worked, untying and retying his bindings. "Next time, keep your mouth shut, eh?"

"Take your elephant-hide whip and beat him!" the Persian said. And the eunuch dutifully laid on with the stiff knotted thongs.

Hasan had determined to maintain silence during the beating, and refuse the magician the satisfaction of his screams, but a cry of agony tore free at the first blow. Hasan had never before experienced such pain. His entire back flamed up with the savage rasp of the rough leather. The second blow fell and he screamed again; the very skin seemed to be wrenched from his body. A third blow, this time across the posteriors— and now he felt the blood running down from the cuts of the lash.

A fourth blow: "Allah!" he screamed. "Protect me!" But there was no protection. A fifth blow; he wrenched up his head and implored the Almighty in the name of Mohammed, the Chosen Prophet—but there was no succor.

A sixth blow. He thought he would faint with the pain, the terrible destruction of his body . . . but he could not faint. Now the tears rolled down his face like the dripping sea water, and in the humiliation and agony he said what he could no longer avoid saying.

"In the name of the Fire: mercy!"

The seventh blow did not fall.

"Raise him up," the Persian said gently. "We shall be eating now."

The slave clothed him again and set him on the chest, and the servant-boys brought wine and boiled rice and set them before him. But Hasan was ashamed of himself—though he had never renounced Allah in spirit—and did penance by fasting. He refused to eat the lowly rice or sip the forbidden beverage.

"You'll eat when you get hungry, boy," Bahram said wisely. "If not today, tomorrow." Hasan knew he was right.

Hasan was kept tied at all times except for meals. He never had a chance to look around the ship, or to talk with the crewmen, though he saw half a dozen of them in the course of their normal duties. It was evident that they feared and disliked the magician, but would not interfere. Undoubtedly they had been hired for such voyages before, or were under regular contract with Bahram, and had learned to ignore the cries and appeals of helpless captives.

Each day the ship coursed south along the Persian shore, farther away from Bassorah and civilization. Each night it hove to in some natural harbor for safety from the demons of night and water. Some days the winds were adverse, and the ship was unable to make significant progress; Hasan blessed Allah for such weather. On other days the winds were fair, and Hasan watched the shore parade by, its rocks and beaches and inlets ever less familiar, in growing despair.

The days became weeks, the weeks months, or so it seemed to one who had no accurate way to reckon time. Hasan also bemoaned the fact that he was unable to perform the required ablutions and prayers. First, the Persian would have beaten him again if he had attempted any obvious homage to Allah, and he did not feel strong enough to undergo such pain the prescribed five times each day. Second, he could be certain of neither the precise time of day nor the direction of the Holy City, which he had to face during prayer. Third, he had no water with which to cleanse himself before prayer. Fourth, he was constantly bound, and could not accomplish the motions and gestures of the normal ritual. He felt unclean and defiled, but there was nothing he could do, and after a time he ceased to worry about it unduly. Allah was all-powerful and all-knowing; if it was His will that his servant be unable to pray properly, who was Hasan to protest?

The shoreline became mountainous, then leveled off into a steady jungle. Great rivers carried their rich sediment into the sea. At times the shore on the opposite side had been visible, but now, crane his head around as he might, Hasan could see nothing but a blue expanse of sea. He heard the crewmen talking, and knew that the ship was approaching the magical land of Hind. This must be their destination, and the number of his days was dwindling.

"Praise be to Allah," he said to himself fervently. "May he send a wind to dash this vessel away from that shore!"

This time it seemed that his informal prayer was to be answered. In the afternoon a sudden blackness came upon the sky, and the sea grew dark and wild. A strong wind sprang up so quickly that it caught the sail before the crewmen could furl it and blasted the ship away precipitously from land. She rocked and pitched sickeningly and her old timbers creaked; Hasan himself, who had much more to gain than to lose, began to fear for his life. A sailor screamed as the boat yawed and pitched him into the whipping sea; before his friends could help him he was gone. They brought the sail down, somehow, but it was already torn. It would be many days before they could make it serviceable again.

Still the wind rose, screaming through the ancient rigging and smashing sheets of water over the tired deck. Now the rain was marching over the ocean, a nebulous army, and the dark of the storm was closing down upon them. Men ran wildly and uselessly about as planking tore loose from the deck and upended into the liquid melee. There was little they could do now except hold on and pray.

Hasan, still bound, was helpless—but he seemed to be in no more trouble than the others. They all were prisoners for the time being.

Suddenly the stout captain worked his way to the space where Hasan lay and the dampened Persian clung with his two boys and the eunuch. "By Allah!" the captain swore, "this is all because of that fair youth you are mistreating. Let him go, and the wrath of God will abate."

"Mind your own business!" Bahram screamed at him. "This youth is mine, and I will not tolerate any interference. Go secure the ship; that's the only way you can save us all."

The captain made as if to release Hasan himself, but the eunuch, at a sign from Bahram, interposed. The captain withdrew, grumbling.

For a moment the sea calmed. Then there was a scream of fear. Hasan looked out over the water where a crewman pointed and beheld a monstrous and terrifying shape. It was an enormous funnel, tiny where it touched the water, but whirling up into a black cloud as big as the sky. High-pitched thunder came from it, a sustained scream like that of a savage sandstorm.

"A marid!" the captain exclaimed, naming the most powerful of the tribes of jinn. "Now we are lost indeed!"

Every person watched, fascinated, as that awful creature waltzed across the ocean, now leaning toward the ship, now artfully retreating. In a moment it would tire of its game and descend upon the ship and tear it apart and smash the fragments, wood, cloth, bone, into the hungry wake.

"Kill the magician!" the captain cried. "He is responsible for this. Appease that marid!"

The crewmen rushed upon Bahram in a body. The Persian drove them back temporarily with threats and demoniac gestures, for they were all afraid of him still, and the big eunuch got between them again. Three men bore him down; a knife flashed, the ship rocked, and suddenly the slave was crawling across the deck, bleeding from a gut wound. Once more the ship pitched, and he rolled over the edge of the deck and disappeared.

The two young servants screamed and tried to escape. They too were caught and sacrificed. Only the Persian himself remained, as the crewmen gathered to bring down the last of the supernatural's grievances. As they delayed, in a larger swell of the sea that forced them all to cling frantically to the tenuous woodwork, Bahram somehow made his way to Hasan and cut his ties.

"It was a mistake, my son," he shouted through the gale. "I do not mean to sacrifice you. Come, I will dress you in fine raiment and take you back to your native land. We are friends!"

The marid lifted its tail into itself and whirled back into the clouds. It had spared the ship. The wind eased and the waves subsided. "You see!" Bahram harangued the crewmen. "There is no quarrel between me and Allah; none between me and this fair lad. The marid was only passing by, and you chose to interpret this as divine intent. You are attacking us for nothing!" And he put his arm around Hasan and kissed him on the cheek.

The captain hesitated. "Is this true, O man of Bassorah?"

Hasan was too confused by the storm and the abrupt change in his situation to answer immediately. "Of course it's true!" shouted the Persian, instilling belief by the power of his voice. "The marid has gone and Allah has made the water quiet. What other evidence do you need?"

Still the captain hesitated, fingering his knife. He was not, in the clutch, a timid man, and he did not change his mind easily. "I want an answer of the boy, the one you have tied and beaten."

Hasan gathered his wits. Certainly he could never trust the Persian again, and would be foolish to throw away this chance to eliminate him permanently. One word would do it—

He opened his mouth, but Bahram spoke first, directly and compellingly. "O my son, in the name of Allah, forgive me for the evil I have done you and do not seek revenge. Let me prove to you how sure a friend I can be. I repent my cruelty to you, and wish only to make amends."

Hasan had thought he hated this man, but there was something so touching and persuasive about the magician's present appeal that he knew he could not go through with it.

"You see," Bahram shouted immediately to the crew, "*he* does not wish my end. Forget the matter and go about your business!" And the captain, an honest but uncertain man, in the face of Hasan's silence, obeyed.

Things were considerably more pleasant after that. Hasan was provided with good clothing and permitted to perform his ablutions in the prescribed manner. Several members of the crew joined him every day.

Bahram said no more about fire worship, though he did not honor Allah either. Everyone was friendly now and Hasan learned many things about the structure and handling of a ship.

Several days were required to repair the sail and the other damaged sections of the ship. Hasan was anxious to commence the journey home, but somehow, in those idle days, he found himself agreeing to Bahram's proposal that they proceed to the original destination.

"O my son, surely you don't believe that I ever intended you evil? I was only testing you in order to be certain that you were indeed a devout servant of Allah and a fit match for my lovely daughter. Only in the heat of the fire can the surest sword be tempered. And you have vindicated yourself gloriously! How can you give up the marvelous adventures that await you, now that you have proven your right to them? Do you want them to laugh in Bassorah and say 'Hasan journeyed three months, but changed his mind in sight of adventure'?"

"What adventure is this?" Hasan asked cautiously.

"O my son, we are bound for the Mountain of Clouds, the most magnificent mountain in the world, upon whose summit are the ingredients for the elixir that makes gold. You want to make more elixir don't you?"

"Yes, but—"

"I knew you would agree. I knew you had the heart of an adventurer. Oh, it is a place of rare enchantment and beauty, the like of which few men are privileged to see. You will find it fascinating, this mountain in Serendip."

Hasan looked up from the restless waves. "Seren-dip? You mean the island Sindbad visited?"

"Who?"

"Sindbad the Seaman. He's famous in Bassorah. He—"

Bahram smiled indulgently. "Believe me, Hasan, his name will never be known beyond your city. A common seaman!"

Thus Hasan discovered one day that he had agreed to go on, although he remained leery of the Persian's friendly words. The ship set sail once more for the fabled land Hasan had read about, that nothing now could keep him from: Serendip. Perhaps, on his return, he would pay a call on the seaman. . . .

More weeks passed. They left behind the marvelous country of Hind, where monstrous elephants were said to roam wild, and bore south along a mountainous coast. Finally the land curved again, and they faced the rising sun; then at last the ship bore north. It was as though they had circled the world and were ascending its far side. Then they cut east again, directly out to sea—and new land came into view. Serendip at last!

The green surf broke against shallow islands under the water and sent white breakers foaming onto the beach. Familiar palm trees came up to the shore here and there, but the rest of the scenery was strange. The sands were not white, but colored—pebbles of white and yellow and skyblue and black and every other hue, intermixed with unusual rocks. And in the shallow waters were remarkable fishes, no less color-ful than the stones, and even stranger marine forma-tions. Bahram had been right: this was a land of adventure!

"Oh my son," the Persian said, "make ready, for this is the place we desire. We must go ashore."

Hasan was delighted at the news. He wanted nothing better than to run along that bright beach and to explore the magic landscape beyond. This was a far cry from Bassorah! He could see already that the earth was not brown, but red, as though the blood of a god had colored it. He no longer regretted his decision to continue the voyage.

But he had uneasy thoughts when he observed Bahram making arrangements with the captain, who was to remain behind with the ship and safeguard the goods aboard. He had thought, somehow, that the entire party was coming along, and did not relish the solitary company of the magician. Yet of course the ship could not be destroyed . . . and the land excursion should not take long.

He made up a pack of supplies, and was ready, physically and emotionally, when the time came to jump into the shallow waves and wade ashore.

The adventure had begun!